GOD IS A KILLER

α EDITION

THIS IS AN APOCALYPSE CONFIDENTIAL BOOK
PUBLISHED BY APOCALYPSE CONFIDENTIAL PRESS
www.apocalypse-confidential.com

First Printing, December 2023

Our acknowledgment to Close To The Bone Publishing, who published *God Is a Killer* in 2022, and to Bristol Noir, in which *Blast and Cruise* first appeared..

Book design by Will Waltz.

Cover design by Matthew Revert.

ISBN 979-8-9873662-3-3

CONTENTS

AUTHOR'S NOTE

For most of its life as an unpublished manuscript, *God Is a Killer* was entitled *Bury the Dead*. In my mind, I had old stories of the Bering Land Bridge and bone records showing the origin of civilization when, at some point, a people buried its dead. This signified the end of animal existence, living second to second and driven by appetites. I worked out a long metaphorical approach and sprinkled the novel with references to interment.

This pleasant state of affairs ended when my friend Stephen J. Golds sold a book to Close To The Bone Publishing named *Always the Dead*. I ditched the more contrived symbolism, revised the copy, and called it *God Is a Killer*.

Like the title, the character of MacDougall changed markedly during drafts. At first he was an alien hunter, digging around sites he thought concealed extraterrestrial skeletons. *God Is a Killer* preserves MacDougall's emotional core—hatred, jealousy, anger, fanaticism—while giving him the form of a charismatic cult leader similar to David Koresh.

All roads lead to the ALPHA EDITION. Marvelously reset and redesigned by Apocalypse Confidential book editor Will Waltz, it includes three additional stories: "Blast and Cruise," where an ex-boxer turned drug dealer meets his biggest fans; "Palm Sunday," a phantasmagoric Portuguese mob tale; and "Molting," a social work psycho-noir.

Have no doubt, then, that the novel you hold in your hands is none other than the last word on *God Is a Killer*: the alpha, and the omega.

-MT

ONE

1

At dusk, Terry "Touchdown" Donovan unzipped the tent flap and watched the wind blow through the fir boughs. Under his sleeping bag, he had six thousand dollars in large bills; next to the money, a loaf of bread and a Glock. The revolver he kept unloaded down the front of his jeans.

He yawned, stretched his arms. Wondered if it was safe to walk around the ravine.

For months, Touchdown had cooked meth every evening with Dog Boy and Dan the Nature Man in a barn near Eliot, New Hampshire. But then Sheriff Fitzroy drove over and accused them of stealing his rightful product. No one was happy about it. Least of all Dan. Five minutes later, Dan was dead.

Touchdown lay on his elbows and closed the flap. Rather than take a walk, he decided to go back to sleep.

He woke up a few minutes later, when he heard someone, or some animal, scratching at the outside of his tent. Touchdown reached into his pants, slid the revolver across his chest. He loaded it and swung back the cylinder.

"Dog Boy," he said, "is that you?"

Touchdown waited for a response. He held up the gun, pulled down the zipper—no one.

Then he craned his neck to the left and noticed a man below a beech tree.

"I come bearing the Good News," the man said. "Have you met your Lord and Savior Jesus Christ?"

"Not today," Touchdown said.

"Just a few minutes."

"Let me be nice, all right? I'm trying to be—"

"If you change your mind," the man said, "I'll be around."

The man disappeared behind the beech tree. Touchdown heard boots moving away from the clearing, toward Brompton and the southern woods.

Touchdown had a headache. Wished he'd brought some weed. He didn't want to be alone, pointing a gun at some stranger. It was all wrong.

He knew it was bad. He'd learned there never were any good times.

As Touchdown wondered if Dog Boy left the lab alive, he heard a twig snap.

Ten yards away, under another beech tree, the man sat cross-legged with his eyes closed.

Touchdown said, "I told you to leave."

The man was about forty years old: he had blue eyes and ragged red hair, his face streaked with dirt. He looked more like a drifter than a cop.

"The woods belong to all men," the drifter said. "Not one of us can say, 'I own it.' It was made for you, me, the rest of creation."

"You don't know me."

"That's right," he said. "Not your last name, your hometown, your date of birth, or your Social Security number. But I do know some *things* about you. As two *men*, we have some *things* in common. We were both born of a woman. You ever think about it? In Genesis, Eve is born from Adam's rib. Woman came from man. Now man comes from woman. How do you figure that out?"

"I—uh—don't."

"Do you know Revelation? Of course, we're *losing* time. Believe me, we're all losing. By the way, if you don't *mind*, may I ask if my friend passed through?"

"I think you should—I-I mean—"

"Sit down, son."

What the hell, thought Touchdown.

The cross-legged drifter was on a Jesus trip. Weird but harmless. Dog Boy had time to arrive before nightfall. Rather than draw Forest Service, Touchdown would wait it out. If he listened and nodded a few more minutes, the man would leave him alone.

"You're on vacation, Mister—?"

"Touchdown," he told the drifter. "Hassles from the wife. These days, I'm always leaving town."

"I'll tell you my story. Two days ago, I walked south from Berlin. Now here I sit. Isn't that something?"

The man was a local, some shed-dweller. "You live around here?" said Touchdown.

"In a way, yes. In a way—not yet. A man like you understands man and his law, its enforcement. I got out of prison... Can you guess why they locked me up? Something I didn't even do."

Touchdown nodded at the man. He and the drifter had things in common after all.

"I was a known guy and got framed in Vermont," he said. "Montpelier police said I robbed a liquor store. First, I never robbed a liquor store. Second, I never been to Montpelier. I don't fuck with the Green State."

The man ignored him. "They said I had weapons, Touchdown. If I had a few guns, it was none of their business. I was legal. *Legal* according to the laws of *man...*"

"I hear you. I once—"

"*At that time* I led a tribe, the Eternal Nations in the Wilderness of New England. None holier, none worthier, none closer to the Word. I have *words,* too. Took them from the Book. In the old days, I called myself Cyrus—a king, a great liberator of—"

"Is that the—uh—Bible—?"

"That's the book. But I don't need a king's name to be right and godly. So please, call me MacDougall."

"You were looking for someone?" said Touchdown.

"A friend," MacDougall said. "Like you and me, a believer. Easy to recognize: rubber boots, shaved head. Cream and a razor. *And lo,* it never rusts. See him?"

"No."

Touchdown heard a voice from the tent: "Good one, Mac."

He turned around and saw a skinhead raising the Glock he'd left under his sleeping bag.

"Six grand," the skinhead said. "Moldy bread, plus the piece."

Touchdown put his head in his hands—there never were any good times.

"Take the cash," he said. "Take the gun, whatever you want."

"Reasonable," MacDougall said to the skinhead. "But our friend Touchdown has seen us, hasn't he?"

"Yeah, I'd say so."

"Listen," Touchdown said, "I'm wanted in Bentham County, I'm wanted in five or six others. I'm the last guy who'd talk to the cops."

"But we know you're here under Mount Hamilton," MacDougall said, walking over to Touchdown. "And you know we're here. Small county. How long until Forest Service got you grabbing your ankles?"

"I won't tell them."

MacDougall stepped back through the clearing, to the edge of the woods. "Do you know the Ten Commandments?"

Touchdown wondered: was he quick enough to slip left, pull the revolver, shoot the skinhead? "Sure," he said, touching his belt. "Who doesn't?"

"What's the first commandment?"

"You tell me."

Thou shalt worship no other gods," said MacDougall. "And from it thou shalt not stray. Understand that only God, the ultimate judge, has power over life and death. It's not my right to take a life. Not at all. But since the end is near, here's some wisdom: flee, take refuge, make thine way to a shelter. If you've been chosen, God seats you at His right hand. If not—a big *not*—you burn."

It was Touchdown's moment. But as he swiveled his neck, the Glock went off twice and he felt a terrible burning between his shoulders. He dropped the gun and sank to his knees.

"That was stupid," the skinhead said.

"Please," MacDougall said. "Respect the man."

"It was stupid," the skinhead said. "You want to pretend it was smart?"

Touchdown heard voices, but felt only the fire in his back, as though someone was pouring boiling water on him, and he blacked out.

2

When Touchdown woke, the men were still talking.

"How much," asked MacDougall, "does a wound like that bleed?"

"Depends," the skinhead said. "Size, distance, the fitness of this fucking drifter. I never shot a Glock, not even in the Brotherhood."

"You know entry wounds."

"Not really."

"How much is he going to *bleed*?"

"If we left him here," Brewster said, "he'd never make it to the road. Too many rocks, too much scree. Can't remember the path up the ridge."

"It wouldn't be *justice* leaving him here."

"You going to heal him?"

"Of course not," MacDougall said. "I'll say it's wrong to leave a man flopping in the dirt."

"Shoot him?"

"It would be right."

Touchdown heard the firing pin, then nothing.

3

In the tent, MacDougall flipped through the roll of bills. "The Lord giveth—and giveth—and *giveth* more. The day has brought us fruit, and by that we shall know it. Now, tell me— what's our purpose in life?"

Brewster tried to recall the verses: *"Lord of lords, light of lights, let us be as the two lamps in Revelations which—uh—"*

"Which followed you—"

"Which, uh, followed you until the end of the world. Have mercy upon me, and a small group of people like me—"

"Sleep," said MacDougall.

4

It was almost sunrise. MacDougall and Brewster sat on the bank of the Sagmo River.

"We'll hunt when the light comes," MacDougall told him. "Fifteen minutes."

"I don't have a watch."

"You don't need a watch," MacDougall said. "Look and see if it's light, that's all."

Brewster yawned. He turned over on his side, untied his boot and shook out the pebbles.

"That bum's bread," he said, "was rotten. Two days since we ate real food.

As if killing the guy wasn't bad enough—we aren't full in the belly."

"Did he deserve to live?"

"No, but—"

"Trust in providence," MacDougall said. "Trust, too, in the prophet Mac-Dougall. See how I tracked that drifter? I'm no stranger to it. Years ago, back in North Carolina, I used to shoot squirrels and sell them to the Mexicans. Skinned them, too. I kept the tails on, so they knew they weren't rats."

The sun floated over the mountains. MacDougall snapped off two birch branches, stripped them, and sharpened the ends with his pocketknife. Then he took the vagrant's bread from its wrapper and laid it on a patch of pine needles.

"Six grand," Brewster said. "We could get more money, a lot more—road-side spots are ripe."

"Show faith," MacDougall said. "No sense wasting bullets or making noise. *Get thou off it.* Stay obedient and He will provide bread enough. Think thou on it."

"It's hard," Brewster said, "to even think right now."

A sheriff's cruiser rolled up the path above the river and the two men ducked behind a fir. *"Babylon,"* whispered MacDougall. The car passed the clearing, driving off further down the road to the highway. With the Buick gone, the two cellmates of Berlin Federal resumed their watch. They waited fifteen minutes, maybe thirty—it was hard to tell. Finally, as MacDougall rose to wake his legs, he heard a rustle in the leaves.

"I see it," said Brewster.

MacDougall scanned between the birches, spotted a raccoon. A bottom feeder, he thought. An oversized rat. But if providence delivered a raccoon, he'd eat a raccoon. He believed in the Lord.

MacDougall stepped from tree to tree while it sniffed around the bread. From behind a beech stump, he lunged at the animal and jabbed at it with his stick. The raccoon took off, scurrying on its tiny legs back to the forest.

MacDougall threw his spear in the dirt. He turned to Brewster. "Get that rascal."

"What?"

"Run."

In his suspenders, rubber boots, and camouflage pants, Brewster sprinted up the saddle toward the ravine. Fifty yards back MacDougall jogged past boulders and the old scree. He was too slow to catch vermin and let the skinhead run.

"Brewster!" he called out. "Stay off the ridge."

The two men chased the animal below the edge of the mountain. Out of breath, MacDougall stopped his feet. He leaned forward and placed his palms on his knees. When he looked up, Brewster and the raccoon had disappeared.

A loud thump sounded from the ravine. He heard Brewster cry.

MacDougall walked the ridge in small, measured steps. Halfway down he saw the raccoon sitting beneath a shrub, blinking at him with tiny black eyes.

Nettles and mud clung to Brewster's face. He had tumbled over rocks and heavy brush, and lay on his back a hundred feet from the river. When MacDougall moved closer, he noticed Brewster's left knee was crooked. A bone stuck out of his leg.

"All right, son?"

"Doctor," Brewster said. "I need a goddamn doctor."

"Walk," said MacDougall. "Take up thy pallet."

"Right now?"

In the foothills, the morning breeze felt cool and pleasant; the Sagmo River ran out slowly to the ocean; a blue jay swooped low between birch trees, warbled its song to the wilderness.

"Minute to pray," said MacDougall.

He went to the river and looked up at the cliffs. From the rushes, he heard Brewster moan.

He ignored these petitions.

True, MacDougall told himself, Brewster was dying.

The whole world was dying. For where, in this dying world, in Babylon, lived the real disciples? Where lived the new Andrew, new Peter? Why did God give him Judas, the Silver Pieces Man?

If Brewster now walked to the Eternal Mansion, he would walk due to God's grace, not to forceps, scalpel, or some disease-ridden blood bag. For never would the hands of physicians molest MacDougall or his men.

"Take up thy pallet," said MacDougall, "and walk."

Brewster sat up rubbing his fat fingers against his knee. "Heal me," he said. "You got the power, you're the prophet—the goddamn *prophet*, Mac."

"Yes," MacDougall said. "But I have not the strength. Again the Lord calls me. On the banks of the Sagmo, I shall receive His power."

MacDougall stood on the water's edge and looked across the current. Thirty feet to the opposite bank, three hundred to the woods. Thirty miles to the Eternal Mansion.

A long walk—too long for Silver Pieces Man.

Did he, MacDougall, lack faith in his disciple?

Yes, but even Jesus had only so much faith. Hanging from the Cross, He asked God why He'd been forsaken.

Would God give him a sign?

Hello, Mac.

Elena.

"Brewster's a cripple," MacDougall said, "and he wants a doctor."

Your cripple walks as God commands. What does He command?

"To raise you, the prophet Elena Dunphy, from the dead."

Will you raise me, MacDougall, with this lame-leg on your back?

"No," he said. "I-I won't. My disciple slows me down."

And lo—the Lord commanded it.

Was Brewster a man large in size, crude in manners, slow in learning, bent in knee, pious until the end? No, he was not. Not at all. He was a traitor to the Nations. Silver Pieces Man.

Across the ravine, the blue jay twitted its melody. Slowly to the ocean ran the Sagmo. The air smelled of wet dirt.

MacDougall coughed and squatted down behind Brewster. The skinhead drew a deep breath, rested his head on MacDougall's boot.

"Close your eyes," said MacDougall. "In a moment, you will leave these woods. Think of the Kingdom as we say the Healing Prayer."

Together they intoned the words:

Blessed is the wound
Blessed is the skin

Blessed is the bone
Blessed be the throne
On which He sits.
Blessed is the touch
Blessed is the hand
Blessed is the tongue
Of the Holy One
Who heals us now.
Over time and space
The creator of the race
Rules the world
And all its flesh.
Blessed is the skin
Blessed is the oil
Rubbed on the sores.
Blessed be the door
That opens to health

MacDougall removed his clothes. He reached in his back pocket, checked the revolver. "Y-You stopped," Brewster said. "We got to *keep praying*. Put your fingers on my leg. You got to heal—"

The cylinder held two bullets.

MacDougall wiped his nose and pressed the muzzle against Brewster's forehead.

TWO

In the parlor, Sarah Van Bommel waited by the foot of the stairs. "Are you ready?" she called up to Timmy. "I don't want to get home late. The party's at seven."

"I'm coming," Timmy said.

He held the balustrade with his tiny hand and shuffled downstairs in a fisherman's hat, overalls, and knee-high rubber boots. He stumbled when he reached the second-floor landing.

"All right?" Sarah said.

Timmy got up and smiled. "I'm fine."

Sarah took her keys from the office and the landline rang. The caller had an unlisted number.

"Causeway House Bed and Breakfast. This is Sarah—"

"Van Bommel? The owner of Loon Hill?"

The call sounded like it came from the cockpit of a helicopter. "This is John Rockford. Masters Kennedy and Wharton. Researcher for Lokust Strategies. From Marin to Bentham County. The Loon Hill project. Dundee. Excavation begins Monday. Mr. Lokust's instructions."

Lokust Strategies was an Oakland consulting firm owned by Isaac Lokust, who had agreed to buy Loon Hill from Sarah.

And Rockford? Maybe one of his handlers. In November, Lokust had stayed at Causeway surrounded by eight or nine assistants who chewed their fingers and tapped on company phones during downtime. They trampled one of Timmy's chrysanthemum beds.

Timmy admired his raincoat in the hallway mirror.

"Exactly," Sarah said, "how great?"

"Circling over Loon Hill," he said. "I can see the roof. Lokust insists you assist. Ten minutes."

"I'll be there," she said.

She hung up the phone. Timmy walked in the office with two spinning rods.

"I'm ready," he said.

"We'll go fishing next week."

"But you promised."

"Next week."

"You *promised.*"

"If we go next week, the weather will be nicer."

Timmy frowned at her. "All right."

"Good boy," Sarah said.

2

Above the outcrops of Wolf's Glen, Loon Hill rose two thousand feet over Bentham County. On its southern slope was a wooden frame house and a graveyard with tombstones dating back to the town of Dundee's founding. Its planned excavation was a scandal, especially to a villager named Brad Nash whose ancestors were buried there. On Friday morning, the zoning would be decided at the selectmen's meeting.

At the top of the incline, a thin and slightly hunchbacked man emerged from a helicopter. He straightened his sunglasses, tucked a clipboard to his chest, and trotted across the peak to Sarah.

"Sorry I'm late," she said. "We—"

"A month behind schedule."

"Where's Isaac?"

"Marin County."

"You said he was here."

"He insisted you visit Loon Hill," said Rockford, "which he insisted from Marin County. How are the local politics?"

"Pretty local," Sarah said. "We won't lose tomorrow."

"During the excavation," Rockford added, "the rest of the hill remains untouched. In particular, Mr. Lokust wants to keep the house. He's become interested in *old wood*. In a mechanical age, he finds it comforting."

"Remind me," Sarah said, "about Isaac's interest."

"The visions of a visionary," Rockford said, "are his own business. He chose Loon Hill for its climate, latitude, elevation."

"Yes, of course."

"No neighbors?"

"No."

"Hunters? Miners? Local homeless?"

"Not within a hundred acres."

"Review the PSA," he said. "No hunting within *five hundred acres*—"

Rockford's phone beeped. He slid the clipboard under his arm and looked in a hurry to leave.

In the cockpit, the pilot was asleep. Rockford rapped his knuckles on the glass. The pilot woke up, waved to his man, and began switching the controls for lift-off.

A shot rang out from the bottom of the hill. A second shot followed and a bullet hit the mailbox with a metallic clang.

Sarah peered down from the graveyard. Bradford's brother Hank Nash and Brad Junior were climbing the slope. Both wore brown camouflage and carried hunting rifles.

Hank fiddled with his bolt. "Anyone see a rabbit?"

Rockford dipped his chin, muttered into a small recorder. "*Tribal greeting—firearms...* You told us no hunters."

"He's not a hunter," Sarah said.

"No?" Hank leaned his hip against one of the tombstones. "No one saw the rabbit? Gray and white one? Little bastard kept hopping."

Rockford put a finger to his bottom lip. "Do you live in Bentham County?"

"Yeah," Hank said, grinning at Sarah. "The woman knows me. Damn, every woman in Bentham County knows Hank. My tribe's been here a long time—decades, centuries, shit."

Brad Junior stared at the ground, fidgeting with his jacket zipper. "Can we go home?"

"Your dad told me—"

"Who is the boy's father?" Rockford said.

"Brad Nash," Hank said. "If you're from county, you know the Nashes. Look at this one—'*Maxfield Nash III, father and husband, farmer, hunter, miner, may his soul forever rest in Dundee.*'"

Rockford turned on the recorder: "*Hunters live in clans—protect claims*

with violence, intimidation. Initiation at young age, nine or ten. Research BMI,
disease burden, mutational load, genotypic IQ..."

"I-is that your helicopter?" Brad Junior said.

"It's a civilian model," Rockford said. "The Sobieski S-76C. Mr. Lokust is an investor in the company."

"What's it for?"

Rockford began to describe Lokust's Sobieski to Brad Junior and Sarah turned to Hank Nash. "Harass me," she told him. "Threaten me, shoot rabbits on the hill. Tomorrow you'll lose."

Hank said, "Worry less about Loon Hill, more about that goddamn Causeway House. Didn't I hear Doyle got drunk and drove a backhoe through the wall? It's in a state. Shame if it fell down again, or if someone just blew it up."

Rockford droned on to Brad Junior: "Mr. Lokust requested an aerial map of Bentham County. Permitting wind, weather, flight patterns, I'll be around when digging begins."

The helicopter turned its propeller and Rockford took leave of Sarah and the Nashes. One foot on the landing skid, he looked down at Sarah and yelled, *"Deal with the hunters."*

The Sobieski S-76C flew above the trees, wheeling north to Bretton Woods and the resorts. Three hundred feet below, as Hank and Brad Junior got into their truck, Sarah shouted down to them: "You owe me a new mailbox."

"Don't worry," Hank said. "We know where you live."

THREE

1

The wind blew down the back of Sheriff Fitzroy's neck, and he parked his cruiser in the driveway at Bibeault's Bail Bonds. He had come to see Levesque, Bibeault's bounty hunter.

The previous night, their bookie Dom D'Arcy had stopped in town and waited for the sheriff at the Crazy Nickel Bar.

"Too late for the poker game," Dom had told him.

"Four o'clock flight," said Fitzroy. "Vegas time."

"How was it?" Dom said.

"A week at the Mirage," Fitzroy said. "Ten grand on Monday. Two on Tuesday. Yesterday, I hit nineteen on the wheel and won twenty."

"Then?"

"I checked out of the hotel."

"That's what I taught you," Dom said. "You got some sun, too. These mountain men have deficiencies, lack of vitamins. See it in their fucking faces." Dom yawned, sipped his coffee. "If you were gone all week," he asked, "who ran your crew?"

"Mud season," Fitzroy said. "Thompson and Cherubini split it."

"Not your deputies," Dom said. "The other ones."

"The cooks? They're fine."

"Sure?"

"I called Touchdown," Fitzroy said. "He hadn't gassed himself."

"Levesque ring you?"

"No."

"He's short two weeks," Dom said. "Last time I got paid by his so-called girlfriend. You know he has a kid?"

"Never told me."

"You never asked," Dom said. "He's got secrets. Things no normal person wants to know."

"Who doesn't?"

"Me," Dom said. "But I'm a dying breed. Next month I sort the books in Costa Rica, then I'm gone. Now it's all automated. Digital and shit. Looks like a board meeting. The new guy's Gustavo, drives up from Lawrence. If Levesque stiffs him, he'll come with a bat, pliers, and a power cord."

"Levesque won't like that."

"No shit," Dom said. "I get the deal—the kid gambles, loses, loses some more, then you pay up. But without me, there's no payment plan. No grace period."

"I'll tell him."

"Good," Dom said, handing him an envelope. "You did well with Detroit. At least *somebody* did well with Detroit."

Fitzroy felt his phone: it was Potter, the manager of Dundee Donuts. "Hey, uh, Fitz," he said.

"I'm at the shop. Taking out the trash, and there's, uh—"

"What?"

"A dead guy."

"Shit," Fitzroy said. He was disappointed—he wanted to hear the New York line.

"Leaving?" Dom said.

"Yeah."

"I'll be around Sunday. Remember, Fitz—God hates deadbeats. Go tell your local bondsman."

Fitzroy found Potter in the alley, smoking a cigarette. He pointed at the dead man's Timberland. "See that boot? It was sticking out of the dumpster. I've seen those bridge bums, but never a man face-down in trash."

"He come around the shop?"

"No."

Fitzroy lifted the man's shirt, prodded the mottled wound on his stomach. "Thirty-eight," he said. "Judging by the clothes, I'd say bikers—maybe Zapiens. I'll tape off the lot."

2

The dead man had been no stranger to Fitzroy.

His name was Tom Tom, and he'd worked on Fitzroy's meth line.

Under a sodium light, the sheriff rifled through Tom Tom's jacket, his blood-caked plaid shirt, jeans, contractor boots. Inside the left boot he found an unused syringe. Fitzroy slid off the denim jacket and carefully inspected Tom Tom's forearms—clean. Then he noticed a track mark above Tom Tom's knuckle.

Two blocks down Main Street, he found a battered Ford Focus. Below the front seat was half a kilo of meth. He carefully sealed it in one of the fast-food bags littering the floor and headed back to Dundee Donuts.

At four-thirty, Bobby Syme's ambulance arrived at the curb. Syme ran Dundee's emergency dispatch, funeral parlor, and grave-digging company.

"Bit early," he told the sheriff.

"That's what I was thinking," Fitzroy said.

"Christ, look at this slob. Earrings. Tattoos. Teeth like boiled corn."

"I've seen this guy," his son Donnie said. "Some kind of thief. A few years ago, he robbed an AMT cabin."

"All the same to me," Syme said. "Sooner or later, we get him dug out, stitched up, and puffy. The county's paying for his burial?"

"Burn him," Fitzroy said.

3

Afterwards Fitzroy had sat in his cruiser, gotten a call from Gaucho. He was the lieutenant of a one-percenter biker gang called the Stone Men. "We found the guy."

"Which guy?"

"The guy who killed Tom Tom," said Gaucho. "One of our guys, a new guy—a fucking prospect. Laconia types getting desperate."

"The Stone Men got less selective," Fitzroy said. "Where is he?"

"Tied down in the weight room," Gaucho said. "Two Stroke spotted the dude in a closet, pulling a bullet from his leg with a pair of scissors. Crazy fucker. He had Tom Tom's wallet, and get this—we found a wire."

"Tell the Stone Men," Fitzroy said, "I'm still a friend. I'll swing by the clubhouse after I see the lab."

The meth lab was a nineteenth century barn on three acres of meadow, hidden from the road by rows of beech trees. The stuff was cooked underground in a container called the hot locker, which he'd outfitted with a chimney.

That morning Fitzroy went up the steps and noticed a new deadbolt above the front door lock. He knocked three times. "Open up."

The door slid back on its chain.

Dog Boy mumbled, "Who is it?"

"It's me."

Fitzroy heard the click of a pistol hammer. "Who's *me?*"

"It's Fitz, you idiot," he said. "Where's everyone else?"

"Touchdown and Dan are in the locker. The, uh, hot locker. We're working hard for you, Fitz. Real hard."

"Good," Fitzroy said. "Tell them Daddy's back from the Strip. In five minutes, I want you three sitting at the kitchen table."

The kitchen had wood paneling, a linoleum floor, and a metal folding table draped with a dingy red cloth. On top of the cloth was a loaf of bread, moldy and growing blue and green spots. The cooks wandered into the room and they were in no better shape. Dog Boy and Dan the Nature Man looked pale, strung out; had they been nodding off, too? Track marks above *their* knuckles?

On Monday, Tom Tom had called him at three in the morning and whispered something about bugs in his socks. *Clean up once in a while,* Fitzroy told him.

"All right," he said. "Glad you pikers enjoyed my vacation. Now I'm here and I want answers. First, I want to know who bought the deadbolt."

Pressing his knees against the table, Dog Boy said, "Someone spied on us. Five-ten, solid, hiker type. I don't know—Zapiens, maybe Stone Men. I chased him out to 305 with a Maglite and a Nineteen."

"Did this *hiker* shoot Tom Tom?"

"What?"

"Two hours ago," Fitzroy told them, "Potter found him in a dumpster, face-down in trash and leaking from his belly."

"Tom Tom was touched," Touchdown said. "We never risked it, trying to score from the Stone Men."

Fitzroy tossed an ounce of meth on the table. "Whoever killed Tom Tom," he said, "didn't even know about this bag."

"First time, that ice," Dan said. "I keep mine in the freezer."

"Know anything about *this*?"

Fitzroy slapped down Tom Tom's hypodermic next to the plastic bag. "You assholes riding the horse?" he said. "Maybe it's the Kentucky Derby in here. Hey, Dan—roll up your sleeves."

"Ignore this pig," said Dog Boy.

Dan the Nature Man stared at the syringe. "Come on, Dan," Fitzroy said. "Show me what's left of your skin."

Touchdown sprang up from his chair. "I quit," he said. "I'm tired of it—I'm tired, tired, *tired* being treated like a *roach*."

"You are a roach," Fitzroy said. "I need four hundred ounces by Tuesday, so you and the boys scurry downstairs."

"I quit, too," Dog Boy said.

Fitzroy said, "Hey, Touchdown—"

The sheriff approached the table. Touchdown pulled a revolver from his waist and aimed it at Fitzroy's neck.

Fitzroy smiled and raised his hands. "All right," he said. "I'm the asshole. Maybe you're right to quit. But tell me one thing. Where's the money?"

"Money?" Touchdown said.

"Yeah," Fitzroy said. "You're dealing on the side. My rightful property."

"No fucking money," Touchdown said.

"Buried in the yard?" Fitzroy said. "The bedroom?" He sniffed the dry air: "Kitchen?"

"He knows," Dog Boy said. "He knows, he *knows*. Shoot him, man."

Showing his back to Touchdown, Fitzroy said, "Allow me to reach down my pants." From his rear pocket he took a small bag of brown powder, holding it between his thumb and forefinger.

"Do you know what this is?"

"Shit," Dan said. He snatched the syringe from the table. "Let's—let's do this. Tom Tom's gone, I can't wait—"

"Goddamn it," said Touchdown. "Put that shit away."

"I've got more bags," Fitzroy said to Dan. "Tell me, where's the money?"

Dan fumbled with the plastic wrapper. "It's, it's—"

"Shut up, Dan," Dog Boy said.

"It's in the—in the, uh..."

"Shoot this *fucking* cop," Dog Boy said.

"Tell me," Fitzroy said.

"Don't fucking tell him."

"It's in the, uh, ba—"

Touchdown aimed his gun at Dan the Nature Man and shot him twice in the chest.

The smell of smoke filled the kitchen. Fitzroy tapped his holster. He squeezed the trigger of his Beretta 92 pistol and hit Touchdown just beneath his right nipple. The cook yelped, dropped the revolver on the carpet.

"Just—give it," Dan said. He leaned back in the chair, pressing his fingers around the tiny hole in his flannel shirt.

Fitzroy looked over at Dog Boy. "The breadbox? Bunker? Is..."

Dog Boy kicked over the folding table and slammed Fitzroy against the wall. They both fell to the floor. The sheriff grabbed Dog Boy's boot and punched him three times in the stomach. Dog Boy lay gasping on the peeled linoleum, his long brown hair swept across his face.

The Beretta landed at the foot of the stove. Retrieving it, Fitzroy noticed the screen door was open.

"Where'd he run?" Fitzroy said.

Dog Boy could barely get out the word: *"Cop."*

"No idea?" Fitzroy said. "You really don't know?"

"The mountains," Dog Boy said.

"Which mountain?"

Dog Boy cleared his throat. "Hamilton."

"Good," Fitzroy said. "Where's the money?"

"It's—in the kitchen."

"Where?"

Dog Boy pointed his broken index finger at the breadbox.

Fitzroy kept the Beretta trained on Dog Boy's liver. He walked over to the breadbox, slid up the small door. Inside were dirty needles, a spoon, and a blackened bowl filled with burned matches.

Dog Boy laughed.

"Asshole," Fitzroy said.

Dog Boy laughed even harder.

As Fitzroy stood over Dog Boy, ready to pistol-whip him, the cook wrapped his scabby arms around Fitzroy's leg.

"You understand," Dog Boy said, "we're all sick."

Fitzroy kicked him above the belt. He heard one of Dog Boy's ribs crack. But the cook held tight to his knees.

"It's not right what you're doing," Dog Boy said. "Not right—"

Fitzroy kicked him again. Dog Boy grabbed his ankle and twisted it. The sheriff shook on his legs, wobbled for a second, flopped down next to the table.

Fitzroy got to his feet and felt a chair break over his head.

When he woke, smoke filled his lungs.

Next to the door, the curtains were on fire. He coughed and ran across the kitchen to the porch. At the entrance of the container, the cooks kept a fire extinguisher.

Fitzroy sprayed the alcove until the blaze died out. The fire had not spread to the rest of the house. When he was sure it was safe, he dragged Dan's corpse to his cruiser and threw it in the trunk.

In the kitchen he wiped up the blood, tossed the mop head in the trash, and ripped out the bag. Fitzroy laid it flat in the Buick next to Dan the Nature Man.

He went for a short trip. Five miles west of Dundee, the Brompton quarry sank deep into the ground. Thirty feet down the slide, beside the rainwater pond, he parked next to a cave and turned off the engine. Fitzroy threw the garbage bag against the wall, lifted Dan's body from the trunk and laid it next to the trash.

Above a deep hole, he dumped quicklime on the Nature Man. "Sick?" he said. "Maybe better tomorrow."

He almost swallowed his nicotine lozenge and returned to Eliot.

5

Now it was afternoon, and sitting in the warm, dim office at Bibeault's Bail Bonds, Fitzroy told Levesque that Dog Boy and Touchdown were gone.

"One week in Vegas," said Levesque. "Your whole crew runs off?"

"Snakes."

"Can you trust me?"

"Of course," Fitzroy said. "You owe me too much money. And it's only a couple of junkies. Simple mistake."

"For this mistake, I want double."

Fitzroy popped a lozenge in his mouth. "Why?"

"They're strung out," Levesque said.

"That makes them dangerous?" Fitzroy said. "If nothing else, Dog Boy can't shake his habit. He'll turn up under the bridge."

"Five hundred, two-fifty up front."

"Five, after it's done."

"Six hundred," Levesque said. "Three hundred up front."

"For a simple tail?"

"Look, you come and ask me—"

"I'm asking you," said Fitzroy, "to do a job."

"I already have a job, Fitz. Look around—this is my job. I pay my bills and I don't need your job. I charge whatever I want. You don't like it, go fuck yourself."

"You tell Dom D'Arcy to go fuck himself?"

"What's that groaner got to do with this?"

"You were late last week. Even worse, he said Eliot women paid your debts."

"My business."

"It's my business if Dom or some guy named Gustavo puts you in a wheelchair. How much is each knee worth? 'Three hundred up front'? Remember, I'm your friend. I can get you the three hundred."

"Now it's seven hundred," Levesque said. "Three-fifty up front."

"Three-fifty," he said to the bounty hunter. "Six o'clock?"

6

The Stone Men clubhouse was an old distillery with five garages. Around the garages ran a concrete walkway and a fence of razor wire. The rear deck had plastic furniture, some bonsai trees, a vegetable garden.

Fitzroy parked his Buick. He noticed two cameras above the front door.

A biker named Two Stroke led a pit bull along the fence. Now in his mid-twenties, Two Stroke was a young Stone Man, and only three years ago had been a Stone Boy.

"Look tired, Fitz."

"What's with the feed?"

"Spoonie's idea," Two Stroke said. "He wants to be more professional."

"This isn't professional," Fitzroy said. "He needs to ask me about this shit."

"Tell it to the man."

Fitzroy walked up the steps to the vestibule and heard a scream from one of the garages. "Wait," he said, "is that the guy?"

"Sure isn't Jesus Christ," Two Stroke said. "That's Sticky, the prospect who shot your boy Tom Tom. He's all messed up. Found him in the closet—"

The screaming grew louder until Fitzroy heard a buzzing noise, then silence.

Two Stroke tugged at the dog's lead. "Cattle prod."

"Whatever," said Fitzroy. "Make sure he doesn't pass out."

Inside a black wooden bar ran the length of the lounge. On the bar were ashtrays, rings of keys, and empty bottles of beer; behind it, two fridges and a flat screen television showing a porn film. A sign on the wall read HERE TODAY HERE TOMORROW. Dressed in club colors, five Stone Men smoked cigarettes and played pool in the rear.

"Where's Gaucho?" Fitzroy said.

The pool-playing men stopped their game and stared at him.

"Here," Gaucho said.

He was sitting at a table near the corner window. The bikers called him Gaucho because he looked Spanish, or whatever passed for Spanish in New Hampshire. On his right hand Gaucho wore a gold skull ring, on his neck a large gold crucifix. He tilted a green bandanna over his long black hair.

The pool balls clacked, the bartender emptied the ashtrays. Gaucho sipped his beer. The whole room smelled of stale smoke and disinfectant.

"You put cameras outside? Where the hell is Spoonie?"

"Hey," Gaucho said, "the cameras are fake. I mean, they're real cameras, but there's no feed."

"Look—"

Gaucho yelled to the bartender: "Get the sheriff a pitcher."

"Keg's tapped," the bartender said.

"Go downstairs."

Fitzroy didn't mind a drink; he had a long drive home. "Anyway," he said to Gaucho, "This morning I called you twice. You've been hiding, right when I need you."

"Busy," Gaucho said.

"Bullshit."

"I'm serious," Gaucho said. "Zapiens want our turf near Waterloo. Spoonie's in the Tri-Cities, signing up dealers. Distributing horse."

"Horse?"

"We're selling horse in Canada," Gaucho said. "You should look into horse, it's got a future."

"Not in Bentham County."

"You haven't tried the Mexican stuff. Want some?"

"No."

"Suit yourself."

The bartender handed Fitzroy a glass of beer. It was lukewarm and tasted of dish soap. "Back to your informer," he said. "Sticky, whatever his name is—who is he?"

"Met him at Weirs Beach last year," Gaucho said. "He told us the Zapiens harassed his club. We took him on trial, strictly a demonstration. Straight away this guy acted like a Stone Man. That's why we called him Sticky." Gaucho wiped his mouth with the inlaid gold bracelets on his wrist. "Disgusts me, you know? A brother's betrayal."

"Weight room?"

"Yeah," Gaucho said. "We cleared out some tables. Made a play area. And before he went north, Spoonie produced the tools. Worked on him."

"You sure he shot Tom Tom?"

"He had the money and your boy's stuff. Your boy, uh—"

"Tom Tom."

"Yeah," Gaucho said. "No mistaking your stuff, Fitz. Nice and cloudy. So fine."

"Tell you something else," Fitzroy said. "Last night the Eliot crew bailed. I'm missing Dog Boy and Touchdown."

"What about the other guy, the hippie?"

"Dan the Nature Man?"

"Yeah, Dan."

"Dan's dead."

"Ah, shit," Gaucho said. "I liked him."

"Dog Boy shot him," Fitzroy said. "When I got back from Vegas, the cooks were all strung-out—armless, legless. I yelled and they scattered like roaches."

As Gaucho emptied the pitcher, a slender woman in leathers opened the back door. She sauntered over to the table and slid into Gaucho's lap, almost knocking over Fitzroy's beer.

"My old lady," Gaucho said. "Tell the sheriff your name, lady?"

"Gina."

"How long we been together?"

"A month."

"Sounds like a new old lady," Fitzroy said.

"We met in Fresno," she said. "Some slum near the highway. Gaucho's the reason I moved here."

A few more old ladies, hands and cheeks and skirts smeared with dirt, all walked through the door.

"They've been *gardening*," Gaucho said. "Hey, Gina, make the old ladies wash first. You walk in the club like this?"

Gaucho called for another pitcher of soapy beer while the bartender carried an ammunition belt and two rifles to the bathroom. Gaucho whispered to Fitzroy: "Want to see the snitch?"

7

"If Sticky's got every reason," Fitzroy said, "why's he saying nothing?"

"We got a program," Two Stroke said. "He's guaranteed to squeal."

Fitzroy ran his finger along the cattle prod on the workbench. "Sure," he said. "How long you been zapping him?"

"Four in the morning," Two Stroke said, "but we don't say z. Like, ever. So we've been *sapping* him."

"What do you mean, you don't say z? The letter z?"

"Spoonie says *z* is a Zapiens thing. It's unprofessional."

Gaucho said, "We sap him every hour and he geeks and spurts in the drawer."

"Did he talk at all?"

"He told us to fuck off," Gaucho said. "That was at six. Around eight he told us he wouldn't beg. After ten he tried to escape, so we sapped him again."

Two Stroke spat on the concrete. "I'll stomp him."

"What a smart idea," said Gaucho. "We need him to talk, and you want to stomp him? He has *information*. Something of *value*. And you, fucking Stone Boy, you want to mash his brains?"

They pulled the bottom drawer out from a steel cabinet with COOS COUNTY MORGUE engraved on the front. Fitzroy peeped inside. Sticky was naked and curled up in the corner.

"Yesterday," he said, "you killed one of my cooks. Means you owe me."

The man tilted his head, resting his right temple against the drawer. He moaned and coughed, blinked his eyes.

"Who's your boss?" Fitzroy said. "Who gives you orders?"

Sticky's head drooped. Fitzroy leaned over and loosely wrapped his hand around the man's throat, propping up his chin with his thumb. "Stay with me," said Fitzroy. "Stay awake, just a few minutes. Now, how many times did they sap you?"

"M-m-m-m—"

With his fingertips, Fitzroy turned Sticky's head to his right until the two men faced each other. "Listen," he said, "I'm much nicer than the Stone Men. I'd rather not *sap* you. Once I get a name, we can all go home. Got a home, don't you?"

"It—it—"

"Yes?"

"It was me." He spat on Fitzroy's elbow, swung a fist at his chin. The sheriff took the blow and choked Sticky with both hands. He squeezed until the informer drooled out blood from the sides of his mouth.

"Hey," Gaucho said, "you're killing him—"

"Had it coming," Two Stroke said, "like a fucking rat. Only so long you can *sap* a traitor."

"Come on, Fitz. He might be Zapiens. Feds."

Gaucho looked ready to jump between the two men. Fitzroy released Sticky. The snitch fell back on his elbows inside the drawer. After rolling it shut, they heard him kicking his bare feet
against the steel.

"Quiet," Two Stroke said, "or I'll send in the dog."

"Tight lips," Gaucho said.

"Before I leave," Fitzroy said, "you'll show me those cameras."

"My office." With his steel-toe boot, Gaucho tapped the side of the cabinet. "This one isn't helping at all."

FOUR

1

Sarah searched for Timmy in the yard, shed, parlor, study, kitchen, his bedroom. She gazed out through the bars on Timmy's windows. He'd gone to the river alone.

It started to rain. Sarah put on her brown Limmer boots and walked fifteen minutes north to the Sagmo, where she found a wet and shirtless Timmy shivering on top of a stone basin.

"I'm *fishing*," he said.

"Come down from the rock."

Timmy took a small, tentative step. He began to cry. "I-I don't think so—"

"Stay there," she said. "Fitz will bring the wagon."

"Why didn't we go fishing?"

"I promise we'll go fishing. Wait until Fitz arrives, all right?"

Timmy's right leg twitched and he knocked a few pebbles in the water. They vanished quickly beneath the surface.

"Be completely still," Sarah told him, "and wait—"

Timmy stepped away from her, lost his footing. As he fell, he swung his arms in the air and with a great splash plopped down into the Sagmo.

Kneeling on the bank, Sarah reached out and took Timmy's hand as he thrashed toward the shallows. He clawed at her arms, trying to fight her off.

"Stay up," Sarah said. "Breathe..."

She heaved and pulled him up to the rushes. Timmy dropped his knees in the mud. She lifted his head, took him in her arms. "It's all right," Sarah said. "It's all right."

2

The rain stopped as Sarah and Timmy walked through the forest.

"You said we'd go fishing."

"It's happening more and more," Sarah said. "Last month, you were on the roof. That's why Philippe built new windows."

"I don't like the windows."

"I don't care," she said.

"Why can't I get a pet?" Timmy asked.

"We're moving to Houston," Sarah said. "You can get one in Texas."

"When *exactly* do we move?"

"When Causeway is sold. And the Manchester building is sold. And the—"

"A small pet," he said. "A parakeet."

"They smell."

"I'd make it wear deodorant," Timmy said. "Smell real nice, like those petunias in the dooryard."

Timmy's parents joined the Nations when he was a baby. A few days later, they disappeared.

He was raised and schooled by the tribe. After MacDougall's arrest, he and Sarah were the only ones remaining at the Eternal Mansion; she reverted the house to Causeway, its original name, and ran it as a bed-and-breakfast with Timmy as her gardener.

Sarah wondered if she'd been cruel to deny him an animal. But animals were filthy—cats, dogs, birds, iguanas constantly made waste. It revolted her. She didn't want the presence of decay in her house.

"We'll discuss it," Sarah said.

"Why? I've been ready this whole time."

"A bird stinks," she said. "It squawks all day. It leaves feathers on the settee. It's greasy. Dirty."

"I don't have anyone else."

"We have each other."

"That's not what I meant, he said. "That's not what I meant at all."

"In any case," she said, "the party's at seven tonight. We're already behind schedule."

3

A stretch of woods five by twenty miles, placed between the White Mountain

National Forest and the Great North Woods, Bentham County was by far the smallest of New Hampshire's counties.

The largest house in Bentham County was Causeway, a granite mansion built in the 1850s by a Boston surgeon named Alfred Cause. It stood on a hundred acres of forest near the Sagmo River.

The house had a slate basement and two floors, as well as an L-shaped dining room on its west side. The front door opened to a curved wooden staircase. To the left, a parlor and music room; further left, a reception hall overlooking doors to a kitchen and office, and, to the right of the dining room, a staircase leading to the second floor. Sarah named the bedrooms after local trails: Headley, Francis, Running Creek, Pluto's Cave, Bear Wood, Fillmore, Gregory's Hood, Jackson, White Hawk, Empire.

The nearly complete eastern wing of Causeway curled around the dooryard gardens, which displayed hollyhocks, fall asters, magnolias, poppies, lupine, black irises, and weeping cherry.

To Sarah and Timmy, it was home.

4

The first guests arrived at seven-thirty.

Among them was Fitzroy, who stood almost six feet tall, overweight, with fleshy earlobes and a paunch. His hair and eyebrows were black. Even to social functions, he wore his sheriff's uniform: a felt campaign hat, dark brown shirt, tan pants with brown stripes on the sides, a cordovan basket-weave belt, and brown Oxfords.

"You stopped coming to the house," Sarah said.

Fitzroy sipped his whiskey. "I've taken an interest."

"In what?"

"Law enforcement."

"How cute."

Settling down on the sofa, Timmy cradled a champagne flute filled with ginger ale.

"We have glasses," Sarah said. "Two hundred different glasses, and you choose a Johnston flute?"

"Good glass," he said.

"You all right?" Fitzroy asked Sarah.

She looked up again at the clock. Sarah excused herself and took the flute to the kitchen.

5

The occasion of the party was Philippe's birthday.

Philippe was the eastern wing's contractor. He and his cousins Laurent and Yoann drank beer at the bottom the dining room stairs. All three came from Quebec. The cousins were a rough sort. Sarah had worried about letting them inside the house.

"It's too bad," Philippe said, "you cannot drive to Gaspésie with me tomorrow." He pointed at a map of North America on the wall: it had been drawn after Champlain's journey to New France. "You see, it's right here below the Saint Lawrence. When this was made," he added, "it was mostly puffins."

She kissed his cheek. "Some other time."

"To be honest," Philippe continued, "I am not sure you'd enjoy Gaspésie. It's cold, windy. Mostly puffins."

In the pantry, she and Philippe kissed again.

"You smell like scotch," she said.

"Today I'm forty," said Philippe. "That means forty-one shots of whisky."

Sarah stared out at the window across the kitchen.

"Are you worried about something?"

"Waiting for Gerry Gobelin," she said. "He hasn't shown up."

"Enjoy yourself," he said, pointing at the eastern wing. "We could sleep in there tonight."

"On the floor?"

"You might like it," Philippe said. "Good for the spine. Growing up, Laurent and Yoann shared one bed. Whoever won the fight got to sleep in it. Yoann always lost—that's why he has good posture."

Looking back over the room, Sarah spotted Philippe's cousins at the kitchen table with two other builders. Next to the centerpiece were a dozen cans of Black Label and a bottle of Johnnie Walker Red. Whenever Laurent poured a shot, Yoann snatched it up and drank it, and each time the builders laughed and pounded their place mats.

She peeked over Yoann's shoulder. The men were throwing dice inside a beveled crystal bowl.

In mid-throw, she grabbed it from the table.

The men sneered at Sarah. Laurent gave her a blank stare. All day they had been drinking.

"It's all right," Philippe said.

Sarah set the bowl back on the mantle. He put his hands around her waist.

"No," she said, and gently loosened his grip. "I'll be on the front porch."

She walked to the door and heard Philippe's voice behind her. "That bastard Fitzroy out there? Tell him he took my bottle."

6

Fitzroy was telling Timmy about his mother.

"Three different shots," he said. "Every day."

"I use orgone," Timmy said. "Much as I can, every single day." Curious, he examined Fitzroy's tumbler. "What are you d-drinking?"

"Why?" Fitzroy said. He swirled around the ice in his glass. "Want some scotch?"

"Scotch? I've n-never had it."

Fitzroy handed him the rocks glass. Timmy immediately gulped it down. He pursed his lips like a baby; his eyes grew red and watery. He poured another drink.

"Hold on there, Timmy."

Fitzroy took the whisky from him. Sarah came through in the doorway and gave Timmy a plastic bottle of ginger ale. He sank back into the couch, propped his sneakers on the coffee table.

"No manners," Sarah said.

"But it's a *party*," he said.

"No."

He meekly put his feet on the deck.

Sarah asked Fitzroy about the sheriff's department. "Stressful," he said. "Too many close calls. Eliot types. You can't trust them. Can I even trust myself? Never know if you're in the right, and besides, being right isn't enough."

She put down her glass and heard the air split behind her. A rock pelted the small of her back. Another rock shattered a window. A third hit Timmy below the eye, and he fell howling to the floor.

She heard Hank Nash's voice. "Flatland bitch."

A drunk Yoann, who had been prowling around the doorway, charged down from the porch. Laurent stopped him at the bottom of the stairs. Yoann snarled at his brother, took a swig of Black Label. Together they staggered back inside the house.

"Let the sheriff handle it," Fitzroy said.

He finished his drink and walked over the yard with his flashlight held away from his chest. Using his right hand, he tapped his holster and drew his Beretta. "Nashes out," he yelled.

An engine started behind the woods, next to Route 302.

A few minutes later, Fitzroy wearily walked back to Causeway.

"I'll call Brad tomorrow."

"You'll call him?" Sarah said. "The Nashes broke my windows, and you'll *call* him?"

"Hank is savage," Fitzroy said. "Not a typical Nash. Besides that, he's in a state. The absolute *state* of him. Gives villagers a bad name."

From the kitchen, the sound of more breaking glass. Sarah heard the dining room table fall to the floor.

The oak table was on its side. Shattered goblets and bottles glittered on the tile. Shattered, too, was her beveled crystal bowl.

Rolling around next to the mantle, Yoann held his brother in a headlock. Laurent kicked at Yoann with his heavy rubber boots. An angry Philippe pulled Yoann to his feet. After each broke his hold on the other, the brothers slumped in exhaustion on the marble.

Despite an earlier warning, they lit two cigarettes and began to smoke.

"*Get out*," Sarah said. "All of you."

7

The last of the guests left Causeway. Yoann and Laurent sat in the back of the Silverado. Sarah said they would never again come up the steps. Philippe stood on the porch and told her, "I'll pay for it."

"You're drunk."

"For God's sake, Sarah. It's my birthday."

Philippe looked pathetic, as he leaned against the doorway in his denim jacket and his wrinkled, whisky-stained tie.

"Good night," she said.

Timmy lay with the covers pulled up to his neck. Sarah handed him a hot water bottle. He squinted at her with filmy blue eyes; the skin was swollen and purple over his left brow.

"I don't feel good."

"Let me see."

She reached forward to touch the bruise. Timmy slapped her hand.

"Timmy, you're hurt—"

"People hurt me because of *you*," Timmy said. "Why else did H-H-Hank throw all those rocks?" He began to sniffle and tucked his mouth under the blanket.

"Sometimes—s-s-sometimes I wish you had let me d-die."

"Timmy—"

Again he pushed away her hand.

She got up, turned out the light. "Sleep," she said. "Tomorrow we have guests."

8

Sarah looked away from the shards of the crystal bowl. She swept them in the dustpan. After setting up the table, she taped cardboard over the front windows, threw the door bolt, and went to bed.

FIVE

1

In the bullpen of the Bentham County sheriff's office, Hank Nash slept on a bench. The lights came on. He twitched his shoulders, rubbed his eyes, pawed sweat from his forehead.

"The bench," he said. "It's the goddamn *bench*."

"Three times the limit," said Deputy Jody Thompson.

"I'm your cousin."

"I have others."

The front door opened, rare during mud season, and in walked a man wearing a blue canvas jacket with plaid lining. He had a wide jaw and neat brown hair in a side-part, moving with his arms just brushing his sides.

"Agent Dumfries," he said, showing Thompson his badge. "I'm with the DEA. Is Sheriff Fitzroy here?"

"He left at six," she said. "Can I—"

"Tell me," Dumfries said, "if you can—what is the business of the Bentham County sheriff's department?"

"Not sure what you mean."

"The business of catching criminals?"

Hank bellowed from his cell. "They got me on false charges," he said. "I'm sober, sober. Completely *sober*. I'm a free man, and a Nash, goddamn it."

"He's my cousin," Thompson said to Dumfries. "Most offenders are known to the department. Some are *older* than the department."

"Thank you," he replied. "I'll be back tomorrow."

Dumfries left the office. Hank said, "I bet Fitzroy's got some dirt. Got bags. Never did like the sheriff or his daddy, pulling over lawful drinkers."

"It's the bikers," Thompson said. "Must be the body Potter found. If Dumfries is any sign—"

"It's about your sheriff."

"Oh, Fitz is all right."

"Is he hell."

2

Fitzroy pulled up to his house and saw lights in the living room. It was almost midnight. Recently his mother had been staying up late.

Fitzroy sat in the Buick, popped a nicotine lozenge. He called Deputy Thompson. "Thanks for looking after my mom last week," he said. "Get her meds?"

"Far as I know."

"She doesn't follow Clement's orders. Sure, she never respected him, but the man's a damn *doctor*. Was my brother around?"

"He visited Monday," she said. "They watched The Price is Right. Your mother told me—"

"—That I tried to keep Patrick from her. Christ, you've met him. Back two months, you booked him for loitering. At the gravel store."

"Someone asked for you—someone from the DEA. Pushy kind. Real nice hair."

"What did he want?" Fitzroy said.

"He didn't tell me."

"That's Feds for you."

"I'll write that down," Thompson said. "Oh, I almost forgot: I called in the Ford Focus."

"Ford Focus?"

"The car outside Potter's work."

"You called the staties?"

"I typed a bulletin. I thought—"

"You were following procedure?"

"Well—"

"It's all right," Fitzroy said. "You've been here three months. Do me a favor, deputy, and next time ring me first. We don't want jackboots around here."

Fitzroy came in and found Patrick splayed across on the couch. He wore a sleeveless red shirt over his bony torso.

"Hey, bro," Patrick said. "Glad you dropped by the homestead."

"They boot you from the halfway house?"

"Washing machine broke," he said. "This is my little furlough, you know? I'm doing laundry."

"I remember last time," Fitzroy said. "You and your boy Gaston shot up in the closet."

"Quiet," Patrick whispered. "Mom's sleeping."

Fitzroy raised his voice: "Mom?"

"Fine, man," Patrick said. "I don't need to fucking stay here. Not for this shit."

He got up and slung a green duffle bag over his shoulder.

"Hold on," Fitzroy said.

"What do you think? *Clothes*, man."

Patrick smiled as he handed the duffel to Fitzroy. The sheriff unzipped it and rifled through Patrick's socks, shirts, and underwear. He turned out the side pockets, patted the bag all over with his fingertips, then slid it back across the floor.

"I told you," Patrick said, "I'm clean."

A latch clicked down the hall. The sheriff heard the creak of his mother's door. She hobbled into the room in a gray flannel blanket.

"What's the matter?" she said.

"Sean's home."

"Patrick was just leaving."

"No, no, he should stay."

"Good night, Mom."

3

Fitzroy spat out the lozenge and shook his brother's hand.

"I'm sorry," he said as they stood in the driveway. "You were right, no need to be an asshole. Staying clean isn't easy."

With a slight lisp, Patrick said, "I'm ha-lean. Going to meetings."

"Saw that bottle under the couch," Fitzroy said. "Stay out of the fridge, little bro."

"Shit—you saw that?"

"I'm a cop," Fitzroy said, slapping Patrick's shoulder. "We're related, in case you forgot. And before you hit the road, assuming you walked here—

anything you want to tell me?"

"Uh—no?"

A sudden move of his hand and Fitzroy scruffed his brother's neck like a cat's. "Spit it out," he said. "The pills or whatever you're hiding."

Patrick sighed. He ran his finger over his upper gum. Into his palm, he spat out three white pills wrapped in plastic.

"How many did you steal?" Fitzroy said.

"First time."

Fitzroy laughed.

"I need—I need them, man," Patrick said. "Know how it feels to be *sick*? I'm freezing, then my boots are melting. Tell me where to cop."

"Nothing in lock-up."

Fitzroy shoved Patrick against the hood of the Buick. He twisted the bottom of his left shoulder, snapped open a pair of handcuffs.

"Hands behind your waist," said Fitzroy. "Straighten your arms. *Both of them*. Whatever you do, don't ask for a lawyer..."

4

When Fitzroy returned home, he poured a glass of Highland Cream and sat his mother on the sofa. Her blanket's fringe was dark brown from being dragged on the floor.

"You're in trouble," Fitzroy said.

"Who's in trouble?"

"You let Patrick in the house last week."

"Oh," she said. "Is he coming back?"

"If Patrick visits, I want you to phone me."

"He's your brother."

"You know what he is? Why he came to the house?"

"To see his mother."

Fitzroy laid the three pills on the coffee table.

"I need a glass of water," she said.

Fitzroy came back to the room with the water and his mother's insulin kit.

"I don't feel like a shot," she said.

"It's not optional," he said.

"I don't—"

"Your arm."

In the past few weeks, with practice, his injections had gotten cleaner and more precise.

"Your father wouldn't stick me," she said. "Not in the middle of the night. He'd wait until I felt like it."

"Dad's not around," Fitzroy said.

"He's out late," she said. "Wish he were here, even though he's always been too soft with you. And you were the oldest."

"I was the best."

She asked him to turn on the TV and he shook his head.

"But I was seeing something. Someone. In or out, I don't remember. Came to me one night. Patrick, he just wanted to stay. He said—"

SIX

1

At daybreak, MacDougall set out for the Eternal Mansion. He got lost leaving Loon Hill and next to a beech root laid himself in the dirt.

MacDougall looked up at a tangle of branches. They were knotted and rough, the bark flaking off. They resembled the crown worn by a certain Nazarene.

Elena's voice came to him.

Do you think of me?

"Always."

Keep the Commandments?

"Yes," he cried. "Even in the wilderness."

Ye shall see the Son of man sit on the right hand of power, and coming in the clouds of heaven.

"Elena—"

A ray of sunlight slanted between the trees. MacDougall said a blessing and followed it out of the forest.

2

Brompton was a dead mining town.

In the Fifties, the state bought the land from the Gobelins, who left their crumbling mansion above the Sagmo and moved to Dundee.

All that remained of the Gobelin estate was a warped and weathered fence and a few blackened slats of wood. A hundred feet west of the site stood a sawmill. Hinges, Atlas bottles, pipes, buckets, horseshoes, rusted sardine cans littered the grass.

The air was sticky, smelled of wet leaves and coal.

MacDougall felt the pangs of hunger.

No doubt, he thought, Brompton had been a happy place. MacDougall envisioned miners eating hard tack and stew as they passed around bottles of whiskey. Those men had smoked their corncob pipes, joked, laughed, blasphemed, spilled beer all over their boots.

MacDougall lingered at the bank of the river. From the east, he heard the whirring of helicopter blades. As the wind picked up, he smelled the dirt, mildew, rotting logs, dust on the leaves. All the dusty and rotting world filled his nostrils.

He drew the revolver as the helicopter circled the trees. Those demons with badges would follow him to the end. He walked alone in Satan's realm, the wilderness of New England.

One bullet? King David never faced such odds.

Quickly as it appeared, the chopper turned and shot over the mountains, wheeling west toward Eliot.

3

Half a mile from the highway, MacDougall spied ten men drinking below a suspension bridge.

"Brothers," he shouted, "have you made your decision?"

"Decision?" said a man with greasy black hair. "Big word, guy. Talk like a *real* man."

"Of course," MacDougall said, "I mean your decision for *Christ*. I am ready to preach the Gospel under this bridge. For I am not ashamed. No, never. It is the power of God unto salvation, to the wino first, and also the drunk. Yes, believe me, also the drunk. Speaking of our Savior, does any man know what today is?"

"Who cares," said a fat red-haired man. "You fucking groaner."

Here, MacDougall thought, was a real man: six-and-a-half feet tall, bloated like a boil, drunk on his father's vodka and his grandfather's wine.

"If no one cares," MacDougall said, "there's no piety here. I see dirty knees—didst the dirt come from kneeling in *prayer*?"

"I ain't gay," said the greasy man.

"Listen, brothers, you will hear of the arrest of a prophet, the wielder of Jeremiah, the great new Moses of the Nations. Yes, time to give account. You know what I see here? Believers. I've never seen so many *believers* beneath one bridge."

A man wearing a torn Dartmouth jacket stood up, leaned against the underpass. Nodding his head, he told the men, "I'm gonna be sick."

"Aw, Doyle. Don't stand up so fast."

"With God," MacDougall said, "any man can stand."

The greasy man said, "This guy's a cop."

"Let him speak," said an old man in overalls.

"I'll ask a question," MacDougall said. "How many of you were *born* under this bridge?"

"Not me," said the old man in overalls. "Had a home in Suffolk. Shit, had a job, too, breaking down boxes at the Riviere paper factory."

"Brother," MacDougall said, "I, too, have known loss. I came from the wilderness, trekked along way. Wore out my jacket. Wore out my disciple. You see, my brothers, today I lost a brother in the woods.

"His name was Michael Brewster," MacDougall continued. "For two years, my cellmate, my follower, my friend. We met up in Berlin, working in the prison cafeteria. At first he hated when I spoke the Gospel. This Brewster was a skinhead: hostile, friendless, no love for his neighbor or himself.

"But one day—I remember it, brothers—I told him about my life as a Christian. I told him Jesus was a divider, not a unifier. He cleaved sons from fathers, friends from friends. Jesus came with a *sword*. And I told him that, as a Christian, I awaited the final war against Satan.

"In Bentham County, I had served in that war. As father of the Eternal Nations, I wore my fatigues and ran maneuvers. I littered the trails with tripwires, assembled AR-15s, *cast down my enemies.*

"Brewster was reborn. He was my second-in-command, my loyal Brewster. When he died, yea, I wept. Then I asked myself: would Abraham have admired this disciple? Would he recognize this brother's leap of faith? Of course, because Abraham honors all who honor the covenant.

"And if we honor the covenant, if we serve Him, He gives us the Kingdom. Who below this bridge will serve, in the final days of the world, to win a place in eternity?"

"Serve me first," said the fat red-headed man. "Got a bottle or money or something?"

"Wine," Doyle said. "Where's the wine?"

"We drank it."

Doyle scratched his chest. "Where's the vodka?"

"Big Red has it," said the old man in overalls.

"Damn well keeping it," Big Red said. He took a gulp from a large plastic bottle. "It's running low," he told MacDougall. "Turn water to vodka, I'll serve you finest kind."

"That vodka was mine," Doyle said.

"When you passed out," Big Red said, "you lost the bottle. Try to pull-haul and I'll pummel your ass. No use wasting good Cossack."

"Come, brothers," MacDougall said. "Think of the Kingdom—be brothers. Deep down, we're brothers."

"Go fuck yourself," Doyle said.

Doyle, who was a head shorter than Big Red, stumbled over and stood in front of him. He planted his feet and crossed his arms, with his patchily bearded chin cocked to the left.

"You stole it when I fell asleep," he said. "You don't steal a man's bottle, it's a rule. Even we got *rules*. Goddamn it, give back the Cossack."

"Drank it," Big Red said. "Loved it." He paused and let out a long belch. "I'll puke it up if you want."

"Asshole," said Doyle.

He threw an uppercut at Big Red's stomach. With a single blow from his right hand, Big Red knocked down Doyle and sent him sprawling on his elbows across the grass.

"Nothing worse than a skinny drunk," Big Red said.

Doyle flipped over on his back. He brushed the leaves from his jacket. "Finest kind shithead, you'll give me that bottle."

MacDougall slunk away up the hill and crossed the bridge. After him bellowed Big Red: "Next time bring Cossack!"

SEVEN

1

At the selectmen's meeting, Gerry Gobelin leaned over the podium and held up a brown leather-bound book. "As you can see," he said, "we have a special guest—an original copy of the town charter, drawn up by the founders of Dundee. The cover is embossed calfskin. Real old calf. Can you see it? We brought this here today because it's relevant to Ms. Van Bommel. A request for the, uh, removal—"

"Movement," Sarah said.

"—of the graveyard at Loon Hill. Reading the charter, we find Article XCIIIA, which addresses the issue of graveyard, uh, removal. I quote—*Upon the burial of bodies, their eternal souls shall be given eternal rest, being against the laws of Dundee to disinter their graves or traffic in the movement of spirits.*"

"And there," Gobelin said, "is our decision. The graveyard at Loon Hill remains untouched, undisturbed—let's say, *unexcavated*. Good luck."

Sarah came to the podium and turned to the green-taped page of the charter. Scanning Article XCIIIA, she saw with her own eyes the town of Dundee forbade *traffic in the movement of spirits.* The words were just as Gobelin had said, with bodies spelled *bodeyes*, and below the article an etching of two snakes.

"What just happened?"

"What happened?" Gobelin said, straightening his glasses. "Another meeting. End of a local conflict. In a word, *justice.*"

"It's a joke."

"The selectmen," he told her, indicating the departing Button and Roper, "are finished with Loon Hill, and so is the Town of Dundee."

"What did Brad tell you?"

"Brad withdrew his complaint. Our decision follows the law, which bans spirit-trafficking within town limits."

"What's he *paying* you?"

Gerry Gobelin finished buttoning his jacket. "If you want, take it to court. When and where is your business. As of this morning, the graveyard stays on Loon Hill."

"I need this sale," Sarah said.

"Given what you can and can't afford, it's a possibility."

"Gerry, this isn't the time—"

"Remember the proverb: *With eager greediness, greed destroys the greedy.* We sold Wolf's Glen two years ago. Times were good. But the good times never last, not even in New Hampshire."

She closed the charter. "Like I said, this won't hold up."

Gobelin said, "The law's finished for today."

2

MacDougall trekked south to Gobelin Auto Repair. The waiting room had black and white tiles, behind it a sliding door to the garage.

At the desk sat Rob Gobelin. He rolled forward in his chair. "Mac?"

"Rob the Rifle—how you been? How's your brother Gerry?"

"Good. Real good. You know, I expected you sooner."

MacDougall took a seat on the red leather sofa. It felt nice to sit. "I need a car," he said. "Price no object."

"Wish I could help," Rob said. "I repair cars, Mac. I don't sell them."

"Sure you do," he said. "You selling AR-15s in Brattleboro?"

"I don't—"

"It's me, Rob."

"All right," Rob said. "I do what I can. International auto sales—different types and models, and I'm telling you, lots of buyers in Guinea, Ghana, Ivory Coast, Nigeria. Less so Liberia. If my fence gets delayed, another fence sitting on the prime meridian calls me at two in the morning and says he'll cut off my head with a machete. Figure someone's calling *him* with a fucking machete. Don't know where it starts."

The shop bells jingled on the door and a woman in a brown deputy's uniform came into the room. MacDougall stared at the wall, confident the revolver was fully tucked under his shirttail.

"Hey, Jody." Rob opened the glass door. "I'll get your Buick."

Rob was gone several minutes. MacDougall peeked over his shoulder to find the deputy staring at him.

"You live around here?"

"Years ago," said MacDougall.

"Where did I see you? On television. *Chronicle*?"

"Just a soldier reporting for duty."

"A soldier?"

"Yep. Some long tours."

Rob came back to the waiting room. The deputy looked once more at MacDougall, took her keys, and left the shop. MacDougall was pleased to see her gone. He patted the gun's grip. "Like I said," he told Rob, "I need a car. Price no object."

3

"What is this?"

"It's a jeep," Rob said.

"It's pink."

"It's a pink jeep. It's what I have, Mac."

"Fall off a truck?"

Rob shrugged. "Not my first choice," he said. "Amazing what it sells for in Freetown."

"How are the plates?"

"Clean."

"And this is the only car?"

"Every other ride is in pieces."

"Keys?"

"Five grand," Rob said. "Since it's you, I'm giving a fifty-percent discount." MacDougall turned to his right. He swiftly poked the revolver in Rob's stomach. "Price no object."

"Jesus," Rob said, holding up his hands. "What's with you, Mac? You were gone ten years. Ten minutes ago, we were at my desk, laughing about machetes. Now it's real finest kind."

"I have a deadline," MacDougall said. "If I explained it, you wouldn't believe me, so hand over the motor."

Timmy awoke tired and hungover. His bruise, raised and purple, had swelled and given his right eye a squint. He scratched his hairless belly and dropped the blinds over the windows.

Below the bed were his work clothes: overalls, a white baseball cap, and green Wellingtons. He expected a long day trimming the grass, mixing soil in the planters.

Timmy fastened a towel around his waist and walked out to the shed. Next to a shelf of mason jars stood the orgone accumulator. It was a six-foot wooden cabinet varnished in burgundy, with Medite on top and an interior lined with galvanized sheets of iron. Between the sheets and the wooden boards were seven alternating layers of sheep's wool and steel wool. All of these materials conducted orgone: Dr. Wilhelm Reich's unit of universal energy.

In the past few months, the orgone had grown weaker.

He increased his trips to the shed, ramped up the conductivity. But after each session, he felt no better. He did not feel *good*.

Timmy shut the door, sat down, and draped a blanket behind his neck. The orgone blaster, a hollow metal cable with a funnel, was at his feet. He stripped off the towel. Light streamed through the window. When Tommy heard a faint hum, his forehead began to sweat.

At seven years old, Timmy had worn camouflage, fired rifles, prayed to Elena every night and obeyed Mac's commands. He was a child when the prophet went to prison.

Now he was eighteen and Sarah told Timmy to forget about MacDougall, forget the old times. But the old times had been good. The old holy times. The Nations lived as a family in a big granite house. They loved the Lord, heard the Word, heeded Mac.

Resting his head against one of the steel sheets, Timmy sprayed the orgone blaster up his nose, over his eyes, behind his ears. At last he felt relief.

He sighed and the pain left his swollen face.

After five minutes, he fell asleep.

Someone had spray-painted FLATLAND BITCH on the front of the house.

Sarah called Fitzroy. "That creep—I want him in jail."

"Who?"

"Hank broke my windows. Now he's calling me a bitch in my own door-yard."

"Hank's at Causeway?"

"He sprayed it across the entrance and ran back to Brad's manse. He's wherever he is now, licking himself. What the hell happened with Gerry this morning?"

"No idea."

"You *know* what happened."

Fitzroy said, "Tell me."

Sarah hung up the phone and laid her coat on the sofa. She began cleaning up the graffiti, scrubbing the crudely looped B with a rag half-dipped in thinner.

She ran through the day's schedule: in half an hour, the guests would arrive from Cambridge. If she spent ten minutes wiping the stones, throwing away broken glass, taping over the
windows—

"Hello, Sarah."

MacDougall looked twenty rather than ten years older. His once-bright pink skin was wrinkled and pale, his red hair thinning and dull. He wore a short beard. When he smiled, his teeth were yellow and ringed with dark brown along the gums.

"Remarkable," he said. "You are so soon removed from the Nations unto another gospel... What happened to the Eternal Mansion? To Elena?" he said, pointing a yellowed finger at the eastern wing. "Oh, I know what happened to *her*. She's buried under that that tower of Lucifer. Satan's citadel."

A green minivan came up the drive: the twelve o'clock guests were early.

"If you only knew," MacDougall said, "about the Kingdom. And how little, little time is left."

The minivan parked next to the air pump. Sarah heard one of the doors slide open.

"Leave," she whispered. "Please, just leave."

MacDougall reached inside his jacket, spread a roll of hundred-dollar bills. "I'm staying in the shed," he said, and tossed the money in a plant pot. "We'll talk later about the Nations. I've invited an old friend."

7

The shed had a dirt floor, wooden beams, and a cement wall lined with fertilizer bags. Next to the mason jars, MacDougall noticed a cabinet six feet high and three feet wide. The cabinet wasn't from the old Nations days—it was new. Maybe satanic.

He opened the door to find a naked man asleep in a lawn chair. The little man snored, resting his head against a corrugated metal sheet. His face was familiar. MacDougall realized it was Timmy.

MacDougall leaned forward, stroked Timmy's shoulder. "Wake up, son. The prophet's home."

Timmy jumped back in the chair, his head hitting one of the side panels. He whipped a towel around his waist. "N-no," the little man said. "I've been waiting—"

"—For a sign," MacDougall said. "We would all have a sign, to know the Lord hears us."

"I-I-It's really *you*."

"I'm home. So is the Holy Ghost. The Eternal Nations in the Wilderness of New England are back."

"Why didn't you c-come sooner?"

"I marched through the blackest hole. Against hunger, against death, against Satan himself I marched. And I did arrive at Babylon. I saw Elena's defiled grave. I mean it is an abomination."

"I n-never went to Satan," Timmy said.

"That's right," MacDougall said. "You're a good boy. A believer. As one believer to another, I need you to explain—"

"Explain?"

"Yes—who lives here?"

"Me—m-m-me and Sarah. Sometimes Philippe."

MacDougall released Timmy. "Philippe?"

"He's Sarah's boyfriend."

"Sarah's my wife," said MacDougall. "Who's Philippe?"

"He's a builder. He'll be back, uh—"

"Today?"

"Tomorrow."

"Anyone else living at Causeway?"

"No."

"Do you know the guests?" MacDougall said. "The women in overalls?"

"The guests?" Timmy wiped his hands on the towel and put on his glasses. "What time is it?"

"At all times, it is eleven fifty-nine. You've been observant?"

"Yes."

"Prayed every day?"

"Y—"

"You lying to me?"

"No."

"You prayed? For Sarah to go to hell? *O that my head were fire, and mine eyes burning flames, that I might weep and burn this brothel to the ground!* Listen, Timmy—you can be worldly in the world, enjoy its joys, reason with its reasons, or you can climb to the Kingdom. One way is death, the other eternal life."

"Yes."

"You haven't been pulling, have you? Down there?"

"No."

"Don't *lie* to me, son."

"I swear—never. I use orgone."

MacDougall sputtered: *"Orgone?"*

The little man told MacDougall about Wilhelm Reich, the FBI, the FDA, the American Medical Association—

"The box collects orgone," Timmy said. "Orgone is the, uh, life force—"

'You believe those whited sepulchers?"

"The, uh, President—"

"It belongs to Lucifer," MacDougall said. "We must burn it."

"B-burn it?"

"You've been brought back to earth. A pilgrim drunk, staggering into potholes…"

"But why b-burn it?"

"Are you not God's child? We read scripture and see the Israelites forget God. He sends locusts, plagues, rapine. Murder and whole-scale slaughter. He scours the tribe from the land."

"Is it—"

"Pray to Him," MacDougall said, "and He'll never let you down." He rubbed Timmy's shoulder. "Neither will I."

EIGHT

1

"Can you believe it?"

Deputy Cherubini sat by the dispatch phone, stirring milk into his coffee. "Fitz left me at Dundee Donuts. Potter was too scared to identify his mom, let alone a DB."

"There was a Ford Focus," Thompson said.

Cherubini put down his mug. "Stone Men," he said. "It's the truth—a barn with a chimney in the backyard."

Fitzroy entered the room with a box of donuts. "There's a few chocolate glazed, Jody. I know you hate plain."

"Thanks."

"How's Patrick?"

"Puddle of drool," she said.

"Let him dry out," Fitzroy said.

2

"He's back," Sarah said.

"Hank Nash?"

"Alex MacDougall."

"I thought he was dead," Fitzroy said. "Wandered out of Berlin Federal and no one heard from him. Thought he'd done one of those self-immolation jobs. How'd he get to Causeway?"

"A pink jeep."

Fitzroy laughed.

"It's not funny."

"Our favorite naked wrestler. Has he committed any, uh, crimes?"

"I'm worried."

"About what?"

"He'll pick up where he left off. With Timmy."

"He staying at Causeway?"

"Staying," she said, "unless you kick him out. I need you, Fitz."

"Did he pay?"

"Two thousand dollars."

"For a single night?"

"I think so—he tossed it in a plant pot. He's sleeping in the shed."

"Kick him out when he stops paying."

"Fitz—"

"Look," he said, "I have my own problems. My brother's in jail. DB in a dumpster. Feds around Dundee. Some Lokust lackey looping Bentham County. If MacDougall threatens you or does anything *vaguely* illegal, text me."

"Not good enough."

"It'll have to be," said Fitzroy.

3

"I can't do the job," Levesque told Fitzroy. "Bibeault's coming by the office, so I'm stuck at the desk. He wants to go over the records—what *records*, I'm asking. As for this MacDougall guy, I'll send my crew."

"Crew?"

"What's wrong with having a crew? Outsourcing. My guy Huffy, he's old school. Lives to get paid and go home."

"Whatever," Fitzroy said. "Maybe he's Joe Commando, but I need to meet him first."

Levesque smiled. "I got it, Fitz."

NINE

1

At lunch, MacDougall drank three glasses of water and needed to relieve himself.

Where better, he thought, than above the stone circle, where twelve years ago he'd dumped the body of Sarah's old boyfriend, the unbeliever Daniel Hurley? It had been a pleasure blasting him with a Remington.

MacDougall spat on the ground. He kicked away the stones and watched the stream of piss hit the damp grass. He felt calm, empty. Reborn. A vessel for His will. The ghost of Elena had interceded; she was more powerful than ever.

He zipped up his pants and daydreamed.

When Elena rose from the grave, he thought, what would she look like? As she looked twenty years ago in Boston, her dyed-black hair in a bun, her face pale and round? As she looked during the Nations' migration north? Or as she looked when she died at Causeway, eaten away by cancer? For months, Elena stayed in bed. She grew thin, thinner, thinnest. Her teeth fell out. She turned to wax, melted, died.

She had taken no medicine—MacDougall saw to it—for the sake of her soul. Later her son David tried to challenge him and ended no better than Daniel. Sarah had played her part.

He stood on the far side of the eastern wing. He gazed up in disgust at the tower, as though Satan crouched in the doorway.

In times of pain, he recited the Book of Jeremiah:

"Many pastors have destroyed my vineyard, and they have trodden my portion under foot, they have made my pleasant portion a desolate wilderness.

They have made it desolate, and being desolate it mourneth unto me; the whole land is made desolate, because no man layeth it to heart.

The spoilers have come upon all high places through the wilderness: for the sound of the Lord shall devour from one end of the land even to the other end of the land: no flesh shall have peace.

No flesh shall have peace—." As he whispered the last verse, he opened his eyes and saw a block of granite, wide as a beech tree, propped against the basement door.

With the block, he had no way to reach Elena.

MacDougall placed his palms on the side. He pushed against it. The slab was solid stone, four or five hundred pounds.

He could never move it himself. And unless God somehow started the backhoe on the hill, no tool could flip it. Only the strength of ten—five?—men could budge it.

MacDougall knew five men.

Hadn't he met them under the bridge?

Large, load-carrying men.

Men who needed honest work.

2

The guests were out hiking the foothills. In the sunroom, Sarah sat across from MacDougall at a long walnut table. "Two kinds of law," he said. "The laws of man and the laws of God. Laws of man are born of man. Dust and ashes. We married twelve years ago in the sight of God, under His law. It's the only law that matters. It means we are *husband and wife.*"

Sarah looked above the mantle: the hands on her clock were set to eleven fifty-nine. The clock was gold gilt ormolu with creeping vines and acanthus, a nineteenth century French copy. Sarah removed it from the wall and set the time at two-fifteen.

"You can change the clock," he said, "but you can't—"

"—Change the time. I remember those mantras."

"Mantras?" he said. "Sound like a pagan. But you wanted me back here. If you were scared, you would've left."

"That would work on normal people," she said.

"You knew I'd return," he said," but you're too stubborn for wisdom. You should have sung hosannas when I arrived at the New Jerusalem. Learn respect, for your sake and the boy's. This is serious."

"For God's sake," Sarah said, "leave Timmy alone."

"You have no claim."

"Neither do you. Remember how you shamed him? Manipulated him? You told Timmy Daniel's death was his fault. You told him to *castrate* himself."

"How could a boy come closer to God?"

"He was seven."

"Acts like he's seven now," MacDougall said. "What, you send him to public school?"

"You have no power—"

"You're my wife," MacDougall said, "so I do have the power. Wed on a cool April day, sun piercing the clouds. The Lord smiled upon us. I felt happy, Sarah. Our wedding night would have been the first of our blessed nights together.

"Demons deferred that future. Babylon *broke the gates* of the Eternal Mansion. They stole the shepherd from his flock. A husband away from Sarah Van Bommel.

"I never forgot you in my prayers. Do you see these hands? Twisted with pain, gnarled with sorrow. Did you read the letters I sent to Causeway? I wrote each in the blood of the prophet and mailed it on the back of God's breath. You never replied to a single epistle."

"I read the first," Sarah said. "I threw away the rest."

"How could you be faithless," he said, "not only to me, but to the faithful themselves? How could you forsake the Nations? Or Timmy? Or turn the Eternal Mansion into a *brothel*?"

"It's my house."

"It's no home," MacDougall said. "I'll tell you a story about homes. I left prison and wandered through the Great North Woods around Cushman. I was a rabbit in a hole. For three weeks, I laid my head in a drainage ditch. And in that ditch, I pondered with great worry on the Kingdom. Every morning I wept, every day I prayed, every night I flayed myself in the mud. Yet I received no answer, not from you or the Lord. Fell into groans. Lamentations. I no longer heard God's voice. Did He condemn me to burn?

"I told myself if I were chosen—a prophet like Jeremiah, or a king like Cyrus—I could jump from Flume Gorge and not suffer a scratch. If I weren't among the chosen, if I were a worthless bug, I'd fall to my death. My death would be righteous, justified—one fewer termite...

"That night I slept in my ditch. I dreamed something miraculous. Yes, with a miracle I received my mission. In my dream, Elena Dunphy's ghost told me to raise her from the soil. Her resurrection is my charge. If I fail to raise her by tomorrow night, I pay an eternal price."

"Ridiculous," Sarah said. "It's Elena or someone else—"

"You're an actress," MacDougall said. "Remember your role. We were joined in holy matrimony, under the sight of God. *Ye must listen to me, and so I shall tell ye:* be careful, Sarah, because the Kingdom soon comes."

Sarah got up and slid her seat under the table. "Leave Timmy alone," she said. "The last thing he needs is this prophet routine. You're no prophet. You went to prison for selling guns, not for following God's law."

"You're disgusted," he said. "Why, because Timmy believes in me? He's a full-grown man, Sarah. Time to join the service. If Timmy can't serve the Lord, who can he serve?"

"He doesn't need to serve anyone."

"We are all servants," MacDougall said. "Your master is Mammon. You are your own poisoner, and the poisoner of others. Defiant, greedy, lustful, vain, blasphemous, flatterer to the usurers, host to the satanic, whore to the Babylonians. Treacherous to your friends, murderous to your brothers. The defiling daughter of the Nations, defiler of Elena's grave. In the end, you'll drop so low into hell you'll beg to die."

MacDougall reached under his chair, laid a plastic cooler on the table. "Now, as I promised," he said, "here's your friend."

MacDougall popped open the lid of the cooler. Inside was a human hand—skeletal, yellow, dead grass and soil pinched between the joints. "David Dunphy," he said. "Elena's son. Your more violent admirer. As you can see, old Dave's lost some weight."

Sarah closed the lid. "Oh God," she said. "You—you cut him up?"

"Remember your *role*," he said. "You're guilty of David's death—a crime, Sarah, frowned upon even by Babylon. When the Feds locked me up, I could have told them about the Final Days. I stayed quiet to protect the Nations."

"With Dave," Sarah said, "you'll *remember*, it was self-defense."

"Tell it to the ATF," MacDougall said. "They never heard that story. He tried to grope you in the shed. He knocked you down. You held the shears, you sliced him open. Gutted him like a dead buck. Left him near dead and whimpering in the shed. You are, shall we say, a *perp*? And I have more proof than Dave's bony hand. We had a chat before I carved him up."

MacDougall pressed a button on an old silver Dictaphone. Sarah heard Dave's hoarse, panting voice:

W-What d-do—

Tell me, MacDougall said, *who did this to you.*

Dave let out a scream.

Don't make me touch you. Now, who stabbed you?

It was S-S—

MacDougall pressed the button. "It's twelve years old," he said. "Sounds good to me. Clean, audible."

"Why are you doing this?"

"You're vain," MacDougall said. "The vain are always easy."

The French doors opened. Timmy waddled in the solarium wearing one of Sarah's white bathrobes. He turned around and Sarah saw Timmy had written TIMOTHY ETERNAL NATIONS in
red marker on the back.

"How do I look?" Timmy said. "L-L-Like a Nations man?"

MacDougall beat his chest with his left fist. "Yes, son. Like a God-fearing believer."

3

"Mac."

In his office, Rob Gobelin paced before the glass door. "Christ," he said, "last time you pointed a gun at me. Stole my jeep. Now you want me to buy dynamite?"

"Who said I wanted to buy it?"

"Why?"

"Quarry work."

"Hell," Rob said, "the quarry guys drive through county. They buy a tire or two. Roughnecks use ammonium nitrate and some other shit."

"Where do they get it from?"

"Stone Men."

"Do they know the men under the bridge?"

"They're bikers, one-percenters. They pimp each other's women. Sell horse from here to Saskatoon. If it's horse you want—"

MacDougall said, "Give me the address."

4

MacDougall drove the pink jeep down 305 and passed a brown sign:

THE WHITE MOUNTAINS - LAND OF MANY USES

Every few hundred feet, he saw a yellow sign marking an S-curve, a merger, a percentage of decline. He sped beside the Muddy River campground and came across a highway safety warning:

BUCKLE UP EVERY TIME - LIVE TO DO GREAT THINGS

How many more days, he thought, would the people of New Hampshire live to do *anything*, let alone *great things*? What chance would the star Wormwood give?

A siren blared behind him. MacDougall glanced at the speedometer; he was twenty miles an hour above the limit. He patted his gun and pulled over to the shoulder.

The woman from Gobelin Auto approached the jeep.

"Afternoon," he said.

"Is this your car?"

"Right now—yes."

"License and registration."

"May I ask why you stopped me?"

"Speeding."

"Most people speed, don't they? On a mountain highway. Far from town. If a gun went off by the roadside, who would hear it?"

"License."

MacDougall's thumb stroked the revolver. "You know how Rob does business," he said. "Took the jeep for a test drive. I'm supposed to return it in an hour, or I'm on the hook."

"One more time—"

The deputy's radio crackled. MacDougall heard Fitzroy's voice: *Need you in Eliot. Feds crowding the Sagmo later.*

"I'm on a speeding stop."

A speeding stop? Basin by five-thirty.

The deputy stomped back to her Buick, made a U-turn, and drove off.

MacDougall lowered his speed as he went through the middle of Dundee. He rolled past the Irving station, the kayak store, antiques barn, savings bank, gravel depot, manses with long driveways and palisades.

PLEASE DRIVE WITH COURTESY - IT'S THE NEW HAMPSHIRE WAY

He would ride God's wind—until the end of the road.

5

Outside the clubhouse, MacDougall parked by an oak grove and walked up the drive.

The front and back lots were empty, the entrance padlocked. On the rear deck, MacDougall peered through the blinds: an office with a swivel chair, bookshelves, a wooden desk. On a laptop played a pornographic movie. He saw no Stone Men.

He entered the room and heard a toilet flush, followed by the sound of splashing water.

While the faucet ran, MacDougall drew his revolver and crept over the concrete to the front door.

At the sink stood a man in leathers with long blond hair, washing his bearded face.

MacDougall aimed at the mirror. The man closed off the faucet with shaking fingers and turned around.

MacDougall nodded at the laptop. "Watch that filth?"

"Who doesn't?"

"I don't," said MacDougall.

"Fuck you."

"I'll make it easy—show me the guns, or that's it."

"What's it?"

"Show me the guns," MacDougall said, "I'll let you keep one ball. Otherwise, they're both gone."

"You're not gonna—"

MacDougall pulled the trigger. It was a good shot, right between the biker's legs, and the man fell screaming to the floor. He swung up his knees, covered his groin with his ringed fingers.

MacDougall stood over him and kicked him in the ribs.

He pressed the barrel against the man's temple. "One more time."

"In the garage," he said. "Jesus, the garage."

6

The fifth and last garage was the weight room. MacDougall found benches, bars, a set of dumbbells, two standing heavy bags. On a plastic work bench were a cattle prod, a bottle of hydrogen peroxide, a bandsaw, and a pair of nose pliers. A moan drifted over from the wall. He saw a six-foot steel cabinet with three drawers.

MacDougall rolled out the bottom compartment.

"Please."

"Where are the guns?" MacDougall said.

"The—what—"

"Guns."

The man's head dropped back. He stuck his chin in the air. He was too weak to crawl forward to MacDougall or even move his feet.

MacDougall tried again: "Guns?"

"Guns..."

"Show me the guns."

"Guns?"

"AR-15s. Mossbergs. Remingtons. Sig Sauers. What have you—Uzis."

"W-who are you?"

"You don't know me."

"Get me out, get me—"

He slid back the compartment and closed it shut.

In the rear office, he found One Ball Man writhing on the floor. The biker inched forward on his elbows toward the desk, where MacDougall noticed a Ruger SR9 next to the laptop.

He brushed off the stainless-steel slide, squatted in front of One Ball Man. "Hey," MacDougall said, "I'm talking to you." He wrapped his fingers around the barrel, then feinted a strike at the biker's head. One Ball Man winced, held up his hands. "I'll show myself out."

MacDougall walked down to the pool tables. He beat the Ruger against the rusted bathroom padlock, snapped it off, and pushed open the door.

Inside were racks of shotguns, AR-15s, two semi-automatic AK-47s, a crate of grenades, and half a dozen ammunition belts. In the corner was a digital clock and a small bag of ammonium nitrate.

Down the driveway came a rumble of engines. MacDougall closed the bathroom door. He pulled an AK-47 from the rack, popped the magazine. The front door opened; he heard chatter at the pool tables. When the bar lights turned on, MacDougall looked through the keyhole and watched five Stone Men sit at a table next to the window. The loudest was bearded and well-tanned. His skin looked broiled like a grilled chicken's. After licking his fingers, he teased his curly black hair and tilted a green bandana.

"That cop still in the garage?" the tanned man said. "Who the fuck is he, anyway?"

"Tight lips."

"Loosen his asshole first."

"Flip him over," the tanned man said. "Treat him like a bitch. Make him squeal, grunt, give a shit."

MacDougall kicked open the bathroom door. In turn he shot each Stone Man and shot the tanned man four times; in half a minute, they were all dead or dying.

More lights, more Harleys, more bikers.

The engines turned off. From the front door came a shout: "It's a fucking raid—"

7

MacDougall heard shots—one, two, three, four.

Over the fence, a voice: "Zapien motherfuckers."

"Bet it's Fitz."

"Fitz is clean."

"Is he fuck."

A bullet hit the bar.

Rifle in his hands, MacDougall rose from the floor and glanced across the counter. He was alone in the main room of the clubhouse. Through the front window, he saw trees, gravel, a few Harleys, but no Stone Men.

A hand grabbed his left ankle. A tile next to the beer taps had been slid back—Stone Men were under the floor. MacDougall twisted around his waist, hobbled on his right leg, then landed his hip on the tile. He kicked out with his boot heel until the hand released him.

The back door opened. MacDougall counted four silhouettes. He aimed the AK-47 down the hole, firing three times.

"He shot Dummy!" one of them said.

Two of the Stone Men carried handguns—Rugers, like One Ball Man's.

MacDougall ran behind a wall next to the bar and shot a gray-haired biker in the chest. When the man fell forward, the Stone Men fired their pistols, but the bullets were stopped by solid wood.

The clubhouse was silent. To his right, MacDougall gazed up at a mural of a man resembling the other bikers: portly, stone-faced, dark-haired, bearded, wearing a leather cap and aviators. Below the portrait was a large caption:

SPOONIE - NONE HARDER

"No way out," a biker said.

"Your man's dead," MacDougall told them. "If you want to live—"

A biker with a machete turned the corner and charged at him. MacDougall stepped to the left, fired twice at his chest. The biker dropped to his knees. MacDougall blew a hole in the back of his head.

"That's one of you," he said. He laid the rifle on the floor and crawled to the dead Stone Man. After removing the man's leather jacket, MacDougall went back to the AK-47.

"What would Spoonie do?" shouted MacDougall.

The Stone Men conferred. "He's got Spoonie..."

"Spoonie's in Canada."

"We don't know. Maybe he blasted Spoonie."

"Are you ready?" MacDougall said. "I've got Spoonie over here. I'm bringing him back to you."

"Spoonie..."

MacDougall kicked out his foot. He slid the Stone Man's jacket across the floor, moved a few feet behind it and shot one of the bikers in the belly. He shuffled back behind the wall, just dodging the other biker's bullet. He dropped his rifle and loaded the Ruger.

"You're fucking dead," the man said.

Squaring his shoulders, right side facing the mural, MacDougall turned his chest to the left. At the first sign of the biker, he shot him in the neck. The man fired before he fell and the bullet tore through MacDougall's jacket.

MacDougall spun and dropped to his feet. He lay on the floor with his right leg twitching. But his lower left side was clean and dry; no matter how he prodded, he could not find the wound.

MacDougall reached in his pocket, groped around until he felt a metal object: the revolver. Its barrel was dented but had stopped the bullet.

"Thank you," MacDougall said to the ceiling fan, and blessed himself.

TEN

1

An old Durango pulled up behind the sheriff's office—Levesque's man.

Huffy the Slasher looked about fifty years old, with his brown hair thinning on top and his muttonchops streaked with gray. Despite the warm weather, he wore a green army jacket.

"Thanks for coming," Fitzroy said as Huffy sank in the leather chair. "Drove from Berlin?"

"Yeah," Huffy said. "Anyway, Berlin's where I sleep. I've lived all over the state: Belmont, Rochester, Franklin, Cushman."

"How'd you meet Levesque?"

"A few years ago, he went broke loansharking in Manchester. Helped recover some debts and he sent me more work."

"He tell you about this particular work?"

"Not exactly."

Fitzroy poured two glasses from a bottle of White Horse. "We have a person of interest. Causeway House. You know the place?"

Huffy left the scotch sitting on the desk. "Yeah," he said. "A fine-ass woman lives there."

"That's right," Fitzroy said. "Her name is Sarah Van Bommel, and she's getting harassed by a guy named MacDougall. Ex-husband. Talkative. I want you to find him, goat-tie him, drag him back here. If he can't be goat-tied, shoot him."

"MacDougall packing?"

"If you see a pistol," Fitzroy said, "I'll get you compensated."

"Sounds good."

"One more thing," said Fitzroy, reaching back in the desk. He handed Huffy a knife with six-inch serrated blade and a cross carved on the pommel. "When you see MacDougall," Fitzroy said, "show him this. He'll be delighted to see it."

2

The man introduced himself as Agent Dumfries. "Nice to meet you," he said. "Nice to visit Bentham County, too. How long you been sheriff?"

"Twelve years," said Fitzroy. "This fall, I'm up for re-election. Can't say I've enjoyed every minute."

"Not a single arrest in six months?"

"Bentham County is small."

"How's it been the past few weeks?" Dumfries said. "Anything unusual? I don't mean unusual as in needing federal intervention. Nothing like that. Asking if anything caught your eye."

"Hank Nash used to wash dishes at the resorts. He got caught with a shotgun at the Northern Inn, and after that he'd been trouble. Spent a night in the bullpen. Came around to our way of thinking."

"The name Brentwood Dentiste mean anything?"

"No."

"Dentiste's a friend of mine," Dumfries said. "He worked undercover for the DEA. I'd bring it up with the department, but Dentiste isn't supposed to be in Bentham County. Six months ago, he took a leave of absence. Everyone thinks he went to his mother's in Rhode Island."

"Why'd he tell you?"

"Like I said, Brent's a friend. Last year his wife left him. Being Brent, he didn't marry just any woman, but some old lady he met while spooking the Diablos. I told him it was a mistake. Working undercover like him, as long as he's been undercover—you forget you're a cop.

"A week after his wife left, Brent heard she got with the Stone Men. He called her, followed her—told me all about it—until one day her phone went dead. Brent had no evidence for a RICO warrant, so the department turned him down. Then he went black."

"Think he's alive?"

"You have agents and you have agents. Dentiste was the best goddamn agent I ever saw. But I'd started to give up hope—that is, until yesterday, when the numbers on his old plate came over the line."

"You're worried about your friend," Fitzroy said. "I respect the DEA—"

"I'll be brief," Dumfries said. "After driving around all ten feet of Bentham

County, I've noticed some things. Know the driveway at the Stone Men clubhouse? This morning I parked my car behind Whittaker Road. Between noon and six, I watched every bike that puttered up the drive. I saw your car, sheriff. I saw that brown—"

"Business."

"What business?"

"I'd been on vacation," Fitzroy said. "Went to meet my informants."

"Who are your informants?"

"No comment."

Dumfries smiled at Fitzroy. "Three informants and no arrests," he said. "To be honest, I hate cow country. But before coming here, I gave myself one goal: find Agent Dentiste. I'm staying in Bentham County until I do."

3

Levesque phoned Fitzroy with good news.

"Dog Boy's sleeping at 17 Chestnut Road, with a woman named Kay Shannon. The place is real Eliot."

At quarter to eight, Fitzroy clapped the knocker. He received no answer and knocked again. A young boy, no more than six or seven years old, opened the door.

"Hey," Fitzroy said, "is Mommy home?"

The boy stared at Fitzroy's badge.

"Are you Kay's son?"

"What did she do?" the boy said.

"No one's in trouble," Fitzroy said. "I need to ask your mom a few questions."

The kitchen had wood panels, filthy rugs, peeling linoleum. Cigarette burns on a green carpet. It reeked of ash and rotting food.

In the living room, Kay Shannon sat on the sofa. Her short hair was brown and wiry, and the rolled-up sleeves of her sweater revealed slender insect arms.

"Where's Dog Boy?" Fitzroy said.

Kay stubbed out her cigarette. "Pay me."

"You spoke with Levesque," the sheriff said. "He pays you."

"You're the one in my house."

Fitzroy looked over at the boy. "Hey, little guy," he said as he pointed at his badge, "do you like police? Should Mommy help the police?"

Kay lit another Marlboro. "You're no police."

"Won't waste your time," Fitzroy said. He stepped across the living room to the hallway.

"Hey," Kay said, "you can't—"

The hall was a short passage with three doors. Fitzroy opened the second door and found Dog Boy rolled over in bed. Kay followed him, cursed him, her footsteps closer and louder.

Fitzroy threw the lock. The bedroom smelled even worse than the kitchen. The floor was strewn with wrappers and crumpled paper bags, the cook lying on a pile of blankets with his face turned to the wall.

"Nice place."

He'd brought a hot shot: a mixture of opium and battery acid to inject in Dog Boy's right arm, or foot, or wherever a vein was left.

Fitzroy flipped over Dog Boy: his lips were blue, pulse gone. The bastard had overdosed without anyone's permission, least of all Fitzroy's.

Nothing to do but shut the eyelids.

Pounding on the door, Kay screamed, "Where's my money?"

Fitzroy pulled the latch and stood in front of her.

"I told you," he said, "to get it from Levesque."

"You walk inside my home, you talk to Dog—"

"Talk?"

"You didn't talk to him?"

Fitzroy shook his head.

Kay ran over to the bed: "Wake up, baby, wake up."

In the living room, the boy stood staring at Fitzroy.

"You said you'd pay me," Kay yelled at him.

"I told you—"

Kay waded through the wrappers and plastic cups. Dog Boy lay on his back, his unblinking eyes staring at the fluorescent light.

"I'll talk to the bounty hunter," he said.

Kay began to cry. "Dog Boy's gone. And you're broke."

"Look—"

"Please," Kay said, "*please*. You can wait here in the bedroom."

"No need." He looked in his wallet: two twenties, two fives, and a one. Fitzroy left twenty on the coffee table. He gave five to the boy.

ELEVEN

1

MacDougall hid two AR-15s, a Remington pump-action shotgun, three bags of ammonium nitrate, and a digital clock behind a piece of drywall.

He scanned the Causeway shelves: rows and rows of reds, whites, gins, whiskies. Any bottle would be cherished by the Bridge Men. Vodka would raise their spirits faster than pinot grigio.

He called to the top of the stairs, where Timmy leaned against the banister: "We'll box up a dozen," he said. "Give alms, invite the believers back."

"Mac... You're *bleeding*."

"A scratch," he said. "Got worse from the bugs at Berlin Federal."

"Maybe you n-need a doctor."

"No doctors," MacDougall said. "Go back to the Book, son."

After the sermon, he left Timmy and walked to the Sagmo for his devotions.

2

MacDougall spotted an Army Jacket Man in a hollow. When he got closer, the Army Jacket Man flashed a knife. MacDougall drew his Ruger.

"Go ahead," the man said. "Pull that trigger. I'll gut you like a fish."

MacDougall removed the safety and the man dropped his knife on the grass. "I didn't mean any harm," the Army Jacket Man said. "Mistook you for someone else. A buddy of mine, hunting rabbits."

MacDougall picked up the man's weapon. "Where did you get this?"

"My buddy."

"Is your buddy the sheriff of Bentham County?"

The man paused. "Don't know him."

"That's a shame," MacDougall said. "Fitzroy and I go back a long way. When I last saw him, he put me in a chokehold and dragged me naked from my wedding bed. Before he grabbed me, this very knife lay on my groom's stand. This knife I needed to kill him. This knife I failed to grasp. This knife is the prophet Jeremiah, the slayer of Anathoth. Carver of traitors. Only a pimp like Fitzroy wouldst bestow it upon thee."

"So what?"

"What's your name?" said MacDougall.

"Nobody."

He hit the man's jaw with the grip of his Ruger. "SMMC? FBI? CIA? DEA? ATF?" Again MacDougall hit him. "Ever speak to a prophet? Not with a full set of teeth, I guess. You'll never have that chance again."

3

As MacDougall pulled the body down the ridge, he had to admit the Army Jacket Man—with his scraggly and shedding red hair, skinny arms, and dirty green jacket—more than a little resembled himself.

From the south side of the clearing, Timmy waved to him.

"Just a minute," MacDougall said. "I'm giving someone directions."

4

"Who is that?" Timmy said.

"A drifter," MacDougall said. "You remember that guy asking for directions? He pointed out this body to me. He said, 'Hey, that's guy's sleeping.' Turns out he wasn't sleeping."

"Where'd the other guy go?"

"He ran off—up the hill. Don't know where."

Timmy touched the bloodied mouth of the Army Jacket Man. "What happened to him?"

"He died."

5

"We need to move him," MacDougall said.

"Shouldn't we tell Fitz?"

"We tell Fitz, he'll think we killed the guy. But we didn't."

They dropped the body in the mud and rolled it in the Sagmo.

Watching Army Jacket Man disappear downriver, MacDougall said, "This is our secret."

"Y-yes."

"Good," MacDougall said. He stroked the back of Timmy's robe. "The Nations keep it in the family. We're a family, right? Babylon tried to break us up. Devils. Remember, the devil isn't red—he's white, and sometimes looks just like you."

"What if someone finds him?" Timmy said.

"The devil?"

"The guy we dropped in the river."

"We'll say we don't know him, because we don't."

"Oh."

"That drifter," MacDougall continued, "died from natural causes."

"Yes."

"Tell me, son—on the final day, will the Lord bring forth a Kingdom of peace?"

"Yes."

"Will He return us to the Eternal Mansion?"

"Y-yes."

"Is Causeway a nest of snakes?"

"Well—uh—w-w-what do you mean?"

"I mean Fitzroy, Philippe. That Army Jacket Man. Witness a generation of *vipers*."

"I don't know," Timmy said. "Phil f-fixed my window. Fitzroy's always been a g-g-good..."

MacDougall cupped his palm below the little man's chin. "Timmy," he said, "no time for deliberation. Forget your will if it keeps you from right action. And what does that mean? It means—we burn the nest."

"B-b-burn it?"

"Where do we live? In Bentham County, we are surrounded by demons, but not afraid. We are threatened, but never cowards. Alone, but not forsaken. Dwelling in hell, serving heaven."

"Y-yes."

"Oh, how he waits for damnation, a man who prays yet doubts—suspects, yet strongly believes..."

"Yes, yes, y-y-yes."

And lo, Timmy believed.

6

Sarah walked up the ridge. On top of the hill, MacDougall stood behind Timmy next to the pines. The little man aimed his AR-15 at an owl's nest.

Timmy screeched: *"Hooooooo."*

Sarah yelled over the grass, told him to drop it.

"He's an adult," MacDougall said. "Pulling triggers since he was six. With enough grip to take down Daniel Hurley. It's time he strayed from the apron."

"I need you home, Timmy."

"Tell us," MacDougall said, "what Timmy does at home."

"He gardens."

"Ah," MacDougall said, "Timmy's earned his keep. Toiled long days, sweated under God's sun, planted those seeds and slowly—slowly—grown his garden. But Timmy tills the garden of Man.
Sweats out his essence for a few dollars, a change of sheets."

MacDougall pointed to the field. Hank Nash, dressed in camouflage, stalked a rabbit near a clutch of dead leaves.

"If God commanded it," MacDougall asked Timmy, "could you shoot that rabbit?"

"I—I..."

"You're a hunter," MacDougall said. He held out the AR-15 and gazed expectantly at Timmy.

"Take the rifle."

"The r-rifle?"

"Yes, it's your rifle."

With both hands, Sarah wrested the stock away from MacDougall. She swung up the barrel and her finger pressed against the trigger. The gun fired a single shot on the grass; a second later, a bullet flew up the hill. It snapped off a tree branch behind MacDougall.

The smell of smoke made Sarah gag. She stared down the hill to find Hank

Nash sliding his bolt.

MacDougall laughed. "The rabbit strikes back."

Another bullet hit the tree. MacDougall grabbed the rifle from Sarah and she dropped over the slope, rolling down the hill until it flattened out.

"How about this rabbit?" MacDougall said. He aimed at Hank and squeezed the AR-15's trigger.

Hank sprinted away up the field.

Sarah got to her feet, coughed into her blouse. "We're going home."

"B-but," Timmy said, "we just got here."

"Go with my wife," MacDougall said. "Have no fear. Have nothing but faith we'll be together."

7

The Bridge Men cheered when MacDougall greeted them. He parked Timmy's truck above the bank.

"My savior," said the red-haired man.

"Bearing alms," MacDougall said. He passed out two bottles of vodka. "It is glory to give unto you. Woe unto them that call water wine and wine water; Cossack for Belvedere and Belvedere for Cossack; that put sober for drunk, and drunk for sober. But I must ask sincerely, truly, fervently—how piously do the Bridge Men receive me?"

"Whoa," Doyle said, "he's a cop."

"He's no cop," the red-haired man said. "He's an asshole just like us."

"And God blessed the Bridge Men," MacDougall told them. "He said unto them, be ruthless, and take what is thine, and travel to Causeway, and subdue it; and have dominion over the ghosts, and over the large stone blocking the basement, and every plank of that satanic box—"

After a time of rejoicing, they piled in the truck and drove east to Causeway.

Sitting in the back, surrounded by thirsty disciples at his side and by his feet, MacDougall handed Doyle another bottle of vodka.

"Have a sip," MacDougall said. "It tastes like nothing."

"I'll take it anyway," Doyle said. "Holy shit, this is better than Cossack."

"I've got plenty more," MacDougall said, and pointed at the case: "Belvedere, Talisker, Andalusian white wine."

The truck hit a pothole, bounced back on the road. The bums jostled each other in the rear.

The man they called Big Red leaned over the side and threw up.

"He's just getting started," Doyle said.

Opening another bottle, MacDougall said, "I hope so."

TWELVE

1

The screen door slammed against the wall. Sarah heard a shout and a dozen feet stomping across the tile.

In the doorway, MacDougall stood flanked by five homeless men wearing white sneakers.

One wore the remains of a Dartmouth track jacket, with a ripped lining and a tear down the right sleeve. It was Doyle, the fired contractor who got drunk and drove a backhoe through the eastern wing.

"In God's house," MacDougall said, "all are welcome."

Sarah put down her drink. "You bastard."

"Has charity gone from the Mansion?" MacDougall said. "No room for the poor? These are the true poor. They sleep in the dirt, drink vodka from plastic bottles. They know Hell. A proverb: *Those cry most who are silent.*"

"But at the Eternal Mansion, they find a prelude to the Kingdom. By God's will, the Bridge Men will see the Kingdom made real. Hear the sounds of my brothers, their squeaks, belches from regions still untouched, *if only not by themselves. If a thousand tongues deny them, a thousand mouths shall be tongueless...*"

The vagrants took turns with the drink tray. "Better than Cossack," one said. "Better than Cossack, better than Cossack—"

In the backyard, three men huddled around the granite block. Timmy hauled a fertilizer bag over from the shed.

"Your hero's back," Sarah said. "He brought Doyle and half of Eliot."

Timmy dropped the bag. "They're believers," he told Sarah. "Mac said we need them. And like Mac said, we're going to the Kingdom."

"Get these men out," Sarah said. "Drive them to the sewer."

"Mac b-brought them," the little man said.

A loud cracking sound came from the wing's far side, where vagrants still lingered near the basement. One man drank from two vodka bottles; another lay passed out on the grass.

Sarah saw the granite block toppled. "Business," one said.

"My business," another said, "is drinking this Cossack."

"It ain't Cossack. It's nice."

"Hey, you almost got killed."

"That little guy—he told us to move it."

2

Fitzroy left the cruiser at Causeway, loaded his Beretta. At nine, he'd gotten a call saying the house was overrun by MacDougall and a gang of drunks. He told his friends at the Nickel he'd be late for their forty-five game.

On the steps, he found Sarah crying in a white trench coat.

"What took you so long?" she said. "There are *homeless* people inside."

"My brothers," Timmy said.

Fitzroy rounded up the men. They looked like Manchester scroungers, not local at all. "Who's the man in charge?" he said.

"No one."

"Where's the skinny guy?" Fitzroy said. "The one who talks a lot?"

"Out back."

The skinny guy sat in the gazebo, drinking seltzer and directing his charges as they rolled the block.

"Hello, sheriff," MacDougall said.

"Your party?"

"Bible study."

"Super cop," one of the men said.

"Ain't no cop," another replied.

Fitzroy grabbed MacDougall's shoulder and tossed him from the chair. He pulled his arm behind his back, turned his right wrist, cuffed him. Fitzroy led him to the cruiser and heard the rattle of ice in glasses. From the corner of his eye, he saw a congregation of men at the back door.

A fat red-headed man necked a bottle of Riesling. "All of you gentlemen," Fitzroy said, "go inside. In thirty minutes, a van will drive you home."

"Ain't got no home," the red head said, "and I fear no cop."

"He's a cop," a bum said.

"He told us that."

"He's a fucking cop. You act like he's a bum."

"He's no friend."

"He ain't no cop," Big Red said. "He's an asshole just like us."

Big Red dropped his bottle of Riesling and advanced downstairs to Fitzroy.

"The shelter," Fitzroy said. "I'll call a bus."

Big Red punched Fitzroy in the stomach. The crowd of vagrants cheered when he slammed him to the ground and began throttling him with his enormous hands.

"No cop," said Big Red. "No cop..."

"This guy's not a cop," someone said.

"He's just an asshole."

"Assholes are cops, too."

"How's he a cop?"

Sweat dripped on Fitzroy from Big Red's pockmarked face. His breath smelled of rancid fish and vodka. Unable to break the grip, Fitzroy tilted his head back until the two men were eye to eye. He got his knees under Big Red's stomach and pushed up against it.

Big Red moaned, started to retch. "No cop." He rolled back his eyes and stuck out his white tongue. Fitzroy heaved him over on his side.

"Hack," someone said.

"Ugly."

"No cop."

Big Red released Fitzroy's wrist. The sheriff took his Beretta and beat him on the skull. When Big Red tried to bite Fitzroy's fingers, he pounded him again below his left eye.

"No... Cop..."

"I hate cops," someone said.

"He's not a cop."

"Who else does that shit?"

"All right," Fitzroy said. "You guys didn't listen to me. Big Red didn't listen, look at him."

"He's a thug," someone said.

"I'm the sheriff," Fitzroy said.

"He works for the sheriff. Nasty."

The porch was bright, the arbor dark. Fitzroy could barely see the silhouettes of the men.

"What do you think?" he said. "You pack up—"

"No cop."

Big Red tackled Fitzroy from behind and threw him to the dirt. Big Red's left eye was covered in blood: the socket had collapsed, the bruise deep blue.

Timmy ran down the back steps. "Stop it!" he shouted. "You're both believers."

Big Red swung an elbow at Timmy's head. It knocked him down and left him squirming on the grass. Fitzroy punched Big Red's eye an inch above the bone. He felt the pain in his knuckles as they smacked flat against the socket.

Fitzroy looked up. Big Red's eye had sunk back in his skull.

"Tore Big Red a newie," someone said.

"Broke him."

"Never heard a crack like that."

Big Red ripped up grass and daffodils with his thick fingers, whimpering. "No cop, no cop, no cop."

"Look at him," Fitzroy told them.

Fitzroy noticed Big Red was barefoot. The soles of his leathery feet were black. "Go have another whiskey," he said. "Ten minutes."

When Fitzroy returned to the cruiser, MacDougall was gone.

3

Sarah ran down the stairs. The homeless in the kitchen barely stirred, staring at their drinks. She left the Bridge Men and went out to the porch.

"Where's Mac?"

"Somewhere around here," Fitzroy said.

"He *got away*?"

"I'll find him."

Deputy Thompson's white van rattled up the drive. In one of the rear seats sat MacDougall.

"Found a man in handcuffs running to 305," she said. "Tied up his feet."

"Thank God," Fitz said.

"Ugh," said Sarah. "Let's thank someone else."

THIRTEEN

1

Sarah ushered Fitzroy into the parlor. "Sit down," she said, "I never really told you about the Nations. Not even when Mac left."

"I have forty-fives in an hour," he said. "What happened?"

"A few weeks before Elena died, MacDougall killed someone close to me. His name was Daniel Hurley. He was a member of the Nations, too.

"One winter, we had no money and no food. Daniel left on a hunting trip with MacDougall and Timmy. Three days later, they came back with Daniel's body. He had a hole in his chest the size of a watermelon. Mac said Timmy shot him, he was aiming for an owl, but I never doubted it was Mac.

"So we buried him. Mac began lecturing me after prayers. I shouldn't be staring at boys, show my neckline, let my robe get loose."

"And?"

"When Mac became the prophet, he wrote new rules for the Nations. First, all the Nations men made pledges of celibacy. All of their wives were pledged to MacDougall.

"He didn't marry the women all at once—he filmed a bride show. Lined up all the Nations women and inspected us right in the hallway. He stared at our teeth—it was humiliating. But most of the women were excited. He picked a woman named Beth Acton, a widow with scoliosis. She was only a few years younger than Elena. He saved the rest of us for later.

"The Nations men spent their days in the forest while Mac instructed their wives in Revelation, the seven seals, Wormwood, the whore of Babylon. Mac was always looking for enemies. He called them Mammonites, and he set up patrols of 'soldiers'—including Timmy—around the yard. One night they beat up some poachers by the river. Those were the only Mammonites.

"After a month, MacDougall gathered everyone in the parlor. He told us he'd found one of God's lost children. Waved at the office door and in walked a girl no older than fifteen. He said, 'This is Heather, who by the Grace of

God came to our tribe. She has renounced the world and come unto the Eternal Nations.' Heather—that little girl—stood there mortified. The rest of us recited the Nations creed. Mac had rewritten it and added verses about dragons and Jerusalem. Awful. We all joined hands and blessed Heather."

"So what?"

"Mac married her. We never saw Heather again.

"After she vanished, MacDougall began ranting about the Kingdom: trumpets, seas of blood, all the rest. He started selling AR-15s with Rob Gobelin. Then the bust. When Mac left, so did everyone else, until it was me and Timmy."

Fitzroy dropped an ice cube in his glass. "Mac's a dead man."

"Why isn't he dead?"

"He's in lock-up."

"Not good enough," said Sarah.

Fitzroy smiled at her. "Good enough when I see the money."

"For what?" Sarah said. "Mac committed a crime tonight—several, I'm sure. He's not getting out, is he?"

"If there had been no witnesses," Fitzroy said, "he'd be floating down the Sagmo. I have to play the game, Sarah."

"What do you want?"

"That depends." He removed his belt, wrapped it slowly around his hand, and placed it on the table. "I don't visit Causeway as often. You still seeing Philippe?"

2

Fitzroy left at two in the morning. Sarah put on her nightgown and went out to look at the eastern wing. She returned to the kitchen, poured a glass of Chablis, and dialed Philippe's number.

"What is it?" he said.

"Service call."

"What kind of service?"

Sarah told him about the block, the steps, the broken floor.

"Who was it?"

"Doyle."

Philippe yawned. "I believe it."

"The inspection is at noon Monday. Can you make it by six?"

"If I'm still in Quebec?"

"You're not... Are you?"

"Depends on the wage."

"Triple your carpenter's rate."

"I am the carpenter," Philippe said. "In this case, I cannot be bought easily."

"Phil... If you have any feelings..."

"I did," Philippe said. "I still do."

"You'll come tomorrow?"

"Yes."

3

Sarah woke on the divan, realized she'd left Timmy outside. She found him curled up under the porch with a half-empty bottle of scotch.

"Are you all right?"

"I've been drinking," he said.

"Get inside," Sarah said. "It's time for bed. We need another look at that bruise above your eye. The wino with the red hair—"

"It doesn't hurt," Timmy said. "And Mac t-t-told me no band-aids, no ointment."

"You're drunk," she said. "Another reason to stay away from Mac. If his winos don't ruin you, you'll ruin yourself."

"Where'd Mac go?"

"Too many seltzers," Sarah told Timmy. "Mac's sleeping it off at the sheriff's. He'll be safe with Fitz watching him."

"What about the believers?"

"Back to their habitat."

"They coming back to Causeway?"

Timmy finally went upstairs and the house was dead quiet. Sarah sat up exhausted at the kitchen table. Fitzroy had given her a Beretta with four bullets in the magazine, one in the chamber. She was pouring another glass when the driveway lit up.

Sarah heard voices in the backyard. None sounded like MacDougall or the vagrants.

"Flatland bitch is *sleeping*," said one.

Wearing her nightgown, Sarah walked barefoot down to the backyard. Hank Nash and Brad Junior sat beneath the floodlights: Hank knelt beside a gutted deer, smearing a cross of blood on the wall. She aimed the Beretta at the back of his head.

"Uh, Uncle Hank—"

"What?"

"That Sarah isn't sleeping."

"Tell her to scrub that paint off the porch. Real estate types should know frontage. She leaves it up, like some soused and hacking bum."

"Uncle Hank—turn around."

Hank saw the gun. He dropped his knife in the deer's slit belly. "Hey, got the wrong house, probably..."

The Nashes drove away in Hank's truck. "I told you," Brad Junior said, "it was a bad idea."

Thank God, Sarah thought. It was only the Nashes—only children.

FOURTEEN

1

On a bench in the county bullpen, under fluorescent lights, MacDougall sat next to his new friend Patrick.

"Who are you, really?" MacDougall said.

Patrick shivered. "I don't think you know me."

"That's right. I don't *know* your middle name, your hometown, your date of birth, or your Social Security number. But I do know some *things* about you—"

Patrick buried his face in his hands. His cheeks were green, his nose running.

"Hey," MacDougall said, "you passing out again?"

Patrick fell unconscious. MacDougall rummaged through his clothes. After finding nothing but lint and a liquor store receipt, he discovered a syringe in the false bottom of Patrick's sneaker.

Patrick woke up. "Hey—w-what... "

MacDougall pulled out the needle from the syringe. He pressed it with his thumb against one of the bars, bending it about one centimeter from the tip. "Now," he told Patrick, "stick your finger down your throat."

Deputy Cherubini bellowed from the desk: "Quiet time."

"My friend's sick," MacDougall said. "He looks like a fish. Bright blue. Green. His gills are clogged. Flipping him back in the river."

Patrick laid out his legs on the concrete, stared at his hands. "Too cold in here," he said. "My f-fingers—"

Nodding his head forward, Patrick took two woolen gloves from a pocket of his jacket. MacDougall snatched one of the gloves. He waved it in Patrick's face. "If you want to get warmer, or a little less green, you need to leave this cell. If it's urgent, and if everything is now *urgent*, you need *treatment*."

Shaking all over, Patrick closed his eyes. "Now it's boiling."

"Satan is a worm," said MacDougall. "Burrows into your flesh. Rots you out from inside. But I'm a tiller—a seasoned tiller of man—and I'll spade him. I'll chop him in half, Patrick."

Patrick looked at MacDougall with cloudy eyes. "Who are you?"

"The prophet," said MacDougall.

MacDougall slipped the glove on his right hand, shot it into Patrick's mouth. He shifted his index finger around to gag him.

"Visit your bullpen," MacDougall called out. "This fish is wriggling. He's got *worms*. He's awful *sick*, he's having a *seizure*."

MacDougall heard footsteps and flung his glove into the corner of the cell. He pinched the bent needle, sticking the tip through the top of his right hand, then curled his index finger to catch the blood. "Hurry," he pleaded, "this man needs treatment." MacDougall winked at Patrick, who was lying face down on the floor. "A *human life* is in your hands."

Cherubini came to the cage. "Turn around," he said. "Put your hands through the bars. Spread your fingers. Don't try anything dumb, or I'll handcuff Patrick to your ankle."

The cuffs snapped around MacDougall's wrists. He smiled, because the deputy had not seen the needle sticking out below his knuckle.

It took MacDougall fifteen seconds to pick the lock; two seconds to throw down Cherubini, kick the back of his head, knock him unconscious.

By the time Patrick turned over, MacDougall had unlocked the bullpen.

"Run along," MacDougall said. "Get thine ass to a nursery."

2

"Last night," Timmy said, "did I help with the believers?"

"At this hour," said MacDougall, "the Bridge Men are too little. Is it not eleven fifty-nine? Recall Revelation, those two lamps, two bearers of light? *Standing before the God of the earth... These have the power to shut heaven, that it rain not in the days of their prophecy: and have power over waters to turn them to blood, and to smite the earth with all plagues, as often as they will.*

"Soundeth familiar? The prophet is Lamp Number One. There's a very good chance—praise God—you're Number Two."

Timmy was astounded. "Number Two?"

"Think I'd lie? You're elect—you're chosen. Chosen long ago, as a foundling to the Nations."

"I…"

"Will you follow the shepherd?"

"Yes."

"Will you fight with the righteous?"

"Yes."

"With a sword?"

"Y-yes."

"Will you kill?"

"Yes, yes."

"Will you ever ask for a doctor, upon sickness—upon death?"

"No."

"Good," MacDougall said. "You've got a friend." He drew the hunting knife and thrust it down in the mud. "From this hour you will pursue, you will divide the spoil, you will draw your sword, your hand shall destroy your enemies. *You will turn water to blood.* Lo, from this hour, this blade is your Jeremiah."

3

They dug holes along the footpath and around the clearing and up the ridge. At daybreak, Timmy walked back to the house.

MacDougall sat by the stream with scissors, a bar of black soap, and Jeremiah. He splashed his hands in the water, lathered his face.

"This what you want, Elena?" he said. "A clean-shaven man?"

Soaped from ears to chin, MacDougall snipped at his beard with the scissors. The hair was slippery and thick. He tossed the tufts in the river.

"Enough, O Prophets? Or do you forsake me as I shave myself? Give me guidance, Lord. Show me weights on the scale. Will ye give your servant the strength?"

Silence.

He cut off another tuft of hair.

"Please look after Timmy."

Another tuft.

"Give me the vision to see."

He saw his reflection in the water; he'd cut his left cheek. MacDougall grunted and smeared the blood across his neck.

It would be a long last day.

FIFTEEN

In Fitzroy's living room, his mother was watching a house-hunting show. "Stay in bed," he scolded her. "You been watching this shit all morning?"

"All night," she said. "I'd like to live in those houses. Like to see you *stop* me."

A window next to the TV was half-closed. "Did you open that?"

"Open what?"

"The window."

"No."

"Who did?"

"Your father sneaked out to the Nickel," she said. "He's hiding from me. All I want is to be nice to him."

His mother asked for something to eat. Fitzroy boiled her old woman's soup: a packet of noodles, powdered flavoring, and a broth cube. He slipped the bowl on a tray and carried it out to her.

"I was on TV," she said.

"You were on *Let's Make a Deal*. We visited Stephie's brother in Los Angeles."

"It was *The Price is Right*," she said.

"Those shows all look the same."

"Was your father there?"

"He was dead."

"What?"

"Should I start from the beginning? A long, long time ago, in a county not so far away, two people joined together in one flesh. That one flesh had a child—me."

"I asked about your father."

"Gone."

"Where?"

"We buried him in Manchester."

"Years ago," his mother said, "I cheated on him. Met a man in Los Angeles. That's why your father's mad at me, but he didn't know this man—why should he be jealous? A friend of Stephie's family." She raised the bowl of soup to her lips and sipped from it. "How is she?"

"She's in Los Angeles."

"Los Angeles?"

"She left."

"She did?"

"She took Matty."

"Who's Matty?"

Fitzroy closed the window. Now he was thirsty and ready to unscrew a bottle of Highland Cream. "I'll be downstairs," he said.

"Tell your father I won't wait up."

Fitzroy stopped at the door. "Is that all?"

2

It was noon when Fitzroy went inside Northern Bargain; he spotted the grip of a Ruger in Timmy's pocket. The sheriff jogged up and slipped the young man under his arm.

"Hey," Fitzroy said, "let's step outside. Talk."

"But I want—"

"—To come to the parking lot."

A few shoppers stared at them. Fitzroy dragged Timmy out of the store and an old logger clapped his hands. "This generation," the logger said, "is the last."

3

Squeezing Timmy's wrist, Fitzroy pulled him through the ivy-draped dooryard of Causeway. They entered the parlor. Sarah ran across the room and hugged the little man. "God," she said, "you're all right."

"Found him at the drugstore," Fitzroy said. He tossed the unloaded Ruger on the sofa. "Back pocket."

"I came to Dundee," Timmy said, "w-with a sword."

"Go to your room," Sarah said.

"No."

"Fitz, please."

"Too much excitement," Fitzroy said. "Too much MacDougall. Lie down and rest. Soak up some orgone."

"G-g-go to hell."

"Fitz and I," Sarah said, "want what's best."

"I want to go home," Timmy said.

"You are home."

4

"County's headed downhill," Doctor Clement said. He was stitching a three-inch cut over Fitzroy's brow. "Different sorts—all bad."

"Who knows if it's bad," Fitzroy said. "Maybe it's good. Outside investment. Isaac Lokust buys my toolshed for a mil."

"You sound like a flatlander."

"It's a free country."

"That's the problem," Clement said.

5

At Bibeault's Bail Bonds, Kay Shannon's little boy sat on top of a filing cabinet. He was shirtless and wore medical tape around his stomach.

"What's the kid doing here?" Fitzroy said.

"What do you care?" Levesque said.

"Huffy," said Fitzroy. "You told me he was old school."

"He's old."

"Past tense," Fitzroy said. "MacDougall knocked out his teeth, strangled him, and rolled him in the Sagmo. What's left of Huffy floated down to Mount Hamilton."

"I've got other guys."

"I don't want *other guys*," Fitzroy said. "I'm begging you, please—shoot this fucking squatter."

The hallway toilet flushed and Kay walked out of the bathroom.

"Son of a bitch," she said.

"Did you pay her?" Fitzroy said.

"That was your job."

"I gave you money."

"Needed it for other things," Levesque said. "You know what they are, so don't make me explain. You scared my son and he cut himself with a steak knife. Six hours at Bentham Memorial. No goddamn insurance."

"That kid is your *son*? You have a *son* with this woman?"

"Fuck is wrong with that?" Kay said.

Levesque asked Fitzroy to apologize.

"For what?" Fitzroy said.

"You killed Dog Boy. Yelled at Kay. And you frightened little Rodney."

"Call me when she leaves."

6

Cherubini was half-conscious and locked in the broom closet.

"MacDougall?" said Fitzroy.

"He kicked me."

Patrick and MacDougall were gone. No leads from his deputy, who couldn't remember much of the attack. Then Fitzroy got a call from Spoonie.

"I was up north," the biker said, "getting scratch in Kitchener. I ride home and the goddamn club's burned down."

"It blew up," Fitzroy said.

"It's the Zapiens. They'll pay with their fucking Z-asses."

"It wasn't the Zapiens."

"Of course it—"

"I know who blew up the clubhouse—name's MacDougall. Remember the cult a few years back?"

"That AR-15 shit? Righteous. But he's paying for the brothers, just like those Zapiens, Z-ass motherfuckers. Where is he?"

"Drifter type. Set up camp near Causeway. Feds collecting bones at the clubhouse, so cool it."

"I'll cool it when he's prolapsed."

"Good boy."

SIXTEEN

1

Philippe carried a ladder and level to the eastern wing. With Yoann and Laurent, he hauled over the new rails and steps. The brothers stubbed out their cigarettes on the façade, threw them in the mud, and jumped down to the basement.

On the second floor, Sarah watched Philippe from her window.

What had she looked for in him? His arms, legs, shoulders as he swung the hammer? She looked back to the mirror, at the window.

From the site he glanced up at her, and in her nightgown, she was not ashamed...

An hour later, Philippe and Sarah lay together on her bed. He turned over on his side, took a Camel from his pack on the nightstand.

"Not in the Empire Room," said Sarah.

He laughed and put away the cigarette. "You must know," he said, "I did not come here to sleep with you."

"I didn't ask."

"We decided together," he said. "Good. But have you really decided to move? To take Timmy and leave Causeway?"

Sarah smiled and reached over for one of Philippe's cigarettes. "I'm moving. There's your answer."

Now that they'd made love again, how did she feel? She wanted Philippe to hold her; she placed her hand over his chest.

"How was the Gaspé?" she said.

"My father's alive, put it that way."

"Was he a good father?"

"Growing up, I felt differently. He was severe. Always working. If he couldn't work on the boats, he cut peat outside the village. He used to take me and leave me in the stables. It smelled horrible. Maybe it was the best time."

"Not now?"

"Not at all," he said. "But there is hope, if you can depend on someone."

Sarah was too tired to keep her eyes open. She fell asleep under Philippe's arms.

2

Fitzroy cleaned his Beretta. His mother yelled down through the floor. "I'm hurting, Sean."

"We have the blue ones."

"The other pills," she said.

"Your other son stole them."

He went upstairs. When he entered the living room, Fitzroy's mother grabbed his wrist. "It's too little," she said. "You said *these* pills would be just as good."

He left his mother and walked back down to the basement. Fitzroy put the Beretta in his holster, drank a shot of Highland Cream. From a wooden stash box—next to a box of filed-off handguns—he took out a syringe and a small bag of heroin.

"This will work," he told her as he held the spoon over the burner.

"It won't hurt?"

"You get shots every day," Fitzroy said. "One more."

"What is it?"

"A placebo," Fitzroy said.

"A what?"

He sat on the couch and rolled up the sleeve of her tattered turquoise blouse.

"You won't feel pain," he told her. "Trust me. You'll feel good as new."

3

The agents drove in unmarked cars to the burned-out ends of the Stone Men clubhouse. It reeked of smoke, blackened timber, gasoline. Most of the main building was gone. Only the steel and brick garages stood along the walkway, cut off by the fence and mounds of debris.

An agent with a notebook trailed Special Agent Falcone. "This is Tunnell," Falcone told the sheriff. "She's new to the Boston office."

Fitzroy said, "You been to New Hampshire?"

"Never," she said.

"Always a first time."

"My condolences," Dumfries told Fitzroy, "about the Stone Men."

Fitzroy grunted. He placed a nicotine lozenge in his cheek.

"Lozenge man?" Falcone said. "I bought the gum when I gave up Chesterfields. These work?"

"Yeah, but I'm popping every hour."

"Nothing like it," Falcone said, and he took a lozenge from Fitzroy. The special-agent-in-charge was a thin man with chestnut hair and a dark brown mustache. He walked stiffly across the grass, jerking his right foot every few steps.

"I told Dumfries," Fitzroy said, "the Stone Men weren't under investigation."

Falcone said, "Far as we know, they kept out of trouble. Three years in Bentham County. Not a single offense."

"I'll tell you the reason," Dumfries said.

"The Stone Men," said Fitzroy, "are—were—a law-abiding motorcycle club. Not one-percenters."

Dumfries said, "A gift to the community. How many donations to the sheriff's department, on a protection racket?"

"To be honest," Falcone said, "there isn't much to the so-called Stone Men. Small clubs are bullied by one-percenters. I mean, routinely and *harshly*. The Zapiens wanted money. They wanted respect, as we all do."

Beyond the ridge came the sound of bombardment.

"Quarry work," Fitzroy yelled.

"Quaint," Falcone said. He took another lozenge from Fitzroy. "Now, I wanted to tell you, sheriff—Department of the Interior is interested in Bentham County."

"Who from the department?"

"No one in particular. Rumors start in X's office, get off and running to Y, who tells a slightly different version to Z, who works in a federal mailroom as a paid informant of A, B, and C."

"Meaning?"

"The United States is the biggest developer in America. Hard to know what the Department wants with Bentham County—hell, I barely know my own department—but I'd expect changes."

"Hey," Tunnell said, "in the garage, there's some kind of..."

The agents stood in a circle, Falcone and Fitzroy sucking their lozenges. Tunnell pried open the bottom drawer with a crowbar. Brentwood Dentiste looked even paler than he had during his interview.

"I told you," Dumfries said.

"Pulse?" Falcone said.

"He's breathing," Tunnell said.

"Wheel him to the plane," Falcone said. "See if he talks his way out of this one."

SEVENTEEN

1

From a dreamless sleep, Sarah woke to an explosion.

The bedroom shook. Through the window, she saw the eastern wing in ruins: a wall of granite had collapsed, and a pile of plaster, wood, and broken stone buried Philippe up to his waist. Laurent and Yoann, coated in soot, pulled up the debris around him.

"Oh my God."

"Terrorist," Yoann said. "Goddamn Yankee terrorist."

Syme and Sons tried to move Philippe, but a large block, weighing at least two or three hundred pounds, had crushed his right leg and lay on top of him.

Bobby watched his sons roll it over Philippe's shin. They stopped when he screamed, but he told them to continue. "It's broken," he said. "I can feel the bones move."

On Philippe's left side, Yoann, Laurent, and the Symes squatted down at the end of the block and hoisted it over Philippe. When this was done, they strapped him to a gurney and sped off to
Bentham Memorial.

On the highway, Sarah followed. She could barely grip the wheel.

2

MacDougall stood on a hill above the eastern wing. The prills, cold packs, and fertilizer had done their work. He only had to raise Elena.

Only to raise her.

By his estimate, the Nations buried her twenty yards from the driveway. It placed her grave beneath what had recently been the ballroom floor.

Below the foundation MacDougall found solid granite.

With the tip of his shovel, he struck at the stone. The blade made a sharp pinging sound, and the shaft wobbled in his hands. Again he struck. He pushed down hard on the handle until the socket snapped off.

"I would have a sign," he muttered. "A *sign*."

Forget Lazarus?

"No—no, never. Not Elena. You shall be raised."

Man buries the dead. God raises them.

"I never doubted Him."

Today you doubted twice. Will there be a third?

"I'm only a man," MacDougall said. "When Jesus was on the cross, did he not call to His Father and ask why He'd forsaken him?"

Once.

The little man was the problem—Timmy and his accumulator. Before the end of the night, MacDougall told himself, one or the other would burn.

3

No one heard Timmy scream when the wing exploded; the whole time he'd stood next to the window, beating his small fists against the bars.

From the second-floor, he looked at the backyard. He knew Mac roamed the woods and awaited the arrival of Lamp Number Two.

Timmy took his sheet and tied it to the bedspread. With the blade of Jeremiah, he pried open the fasteners on the window bars and sliced through the center of the screen.

He climbed out through the window with his blankets, set the balls of his bare feet on the shingles. Following the gust, he shuffled sideways across the roof.

When he passed the second gable, the wind twisted the sheets in the air. Timmy slid three feet down the valley. He scrambled to his left, stuck his foot beneath the bedspread and crawled up the roof. Then he tied the bedspread around the chimney. He looped the blanket, tugging it twice to make sure the knot was firm.

Timmy stepped back down the incline. He gripped the sheet tightly in his small hands. But as he lifted his foot over the last shingle, the knot untangled around the chimney and the sheets dropped over the side. Timmy swung from the gutter, holding on with his stumpy fingers.

From below came MacDougall's voice.

"What weighs this fall," he said, "against the Fall of Man?"

"W-where are you?"

"You're free to leap. By the way, I told you to keep the fertilizer in the basement. For the Lord's candle."

"I'm sorry."

"Let go," MacDougall said.

The little man dropped and fell into his arms.

4

"Where's Jeremiah?"

"I don't know—"

"Don't know what?"

"I m-must have left Jeremiah upstairs."

"Run," MacDougall said, "fetch the prophet of Anathoth. Be a true Number Two. Retrieve Jeremiah."

5

At Bentham Memorial, the ambulance sped into the parking lot. On the gurney lay Rockford—mouth open, nose mutilated, his left eye impaled by a four-inch shard of glass. Ronnie and Donnie Syme wheeled him up to the ER. Ten minutes later, the two brothers returned to the lobby.

"I know that man," Sarah said.

"Helicopter crash," Ronnie said. "It landed north of Hamilton. Another guy crawled out and ran away. Why you'd run from an ambulance, I have no idea. This one looks dead."

"Nice helicopter," Donnie said.

"That was Rockford," Sarah said.

"Sure," Ronnie said. "He was somebody."

"Never seen his kind," Donnie said. "They've been flying them in?"

"His kind—I mean, his company—was going to buy Loon Hill."

"The graveyard?" Ronnie said. "Good thing it doesn't sell, eh? For your own safety."

"Yes," Sarah said. "Good thing."

EIGHTEEN

1

Sitting on the front porch, MacDougall saw Sarah's car approaching. He looked up to the sky. "Elena?" he said. "Are you there? Beware, it's more than the sheriff. The woman Sarah's here, the wife—I would have a *sign*."

Sarah opened the door and pointed her Beretta at MacDougall.

"Act of God," MacDougall said.

Fitzroy clapped his hands as he walked up the drive. "This time," he said, "you put up a fight. You aren't naked, either. That's an improvement."

MacDougall lifted his shirt, showed them the handle of his Ruger. "Can you squeeze that trigger?" he asked Sarah. "Fire straight?"

Following Fitzroy, Thompson and Cherubini arrived in the yard.

The sheriff said, "Let's make a deal—if you drop that gun, I'll forget the jail break and stick to trespassing. I'll forget the trespassing if you follow my instructions."

"Sure."

MacDougall raised his hands. Timmy walked out to the porch holding Jeremiah. MacDougall stepped back, swung his arm around the little man's throat, and pressed the pistol against his temple.

"Lose the shooter," MacDougall said.

"Let him go."

"What if you miss?"

Sarah pulled the trigger; she had forgotten to switch off the safety.

Keeping Timmy's neck behind his elbow, MacDougall laughed. He pulled the little man back through the doorway.

Fitzroy looked over at Thompson. "How fast are you?"

"You want me to chase him?"

"Get close enough to aim," Fitzroy said.

"But—"

"Go."

"Are you OK?" Fitzroy said to Sarah.

"I don't know," she said. "I tried to shoot Mac. I wanted to kill him. God, I almost hurt Timmy."

Fitzroy put his arm around her: "It's all right. These things—"

"Please," she said, "please, don't touch me."

"Sure," said Fitzroy. "Leave it to the fucking deputies."

2

MacDougall released Timmy and they sprinted up the hill, each Nations man darting across the path in overlapping lines. Fast as she could, Thompson ran a hundred yards behind them.

"Stop," Fitzroy yelled to her. "The boys are running maneuvers."

"What?"

"Shoot that pile of leaves," Fitzroy said.

Thompson watched Timmy and MacDougall disappear over the ridge. "You want me to quit chasing them?"

"Shoot the damn leaves."

Thompson fired and hit a birch tree.

"Again," Fitzroy said.

The bullet hit the patch of leaves, punctured what sounded like a plastic milk jug.

"Again."

Thompson's bullet grazed the target. The milk jug exploded half-way up the hill.

"Rigged these woods," Fitzroy said. "They'll slide their asses down to Wolf's Glen. We'll catch them."

3

Thompson and Cherubini took the Buick to Route 305. After crossing the railroad tracks, the cruiser picked up speed, its wheels tracing a tight curve around eighty-eight acres of Causeway.

But when the deputies left the dirt road, Thompson jerked the wheel and swerved right; the Buick spun off the pavement and rolled twenty feet down the embankment. At last, the car stopped a few feet in front of a beech tree.

"You all right?" Thompson said to Cherubini.

"Remember your training," Cherubini said. "You're supposed to squash them, not pull off the road."

"I'll take that as a yes."

"I'm dizzy," Cherubini said. "MacDougall suckered me in the bullpen. Need to lie down."

Thompson radioed Fitzroy: "We went off that stretch of 305," she said. "Cherubini has a concussion, or something worse."

"I want you in *pursuit*, deputy."

"Sorry, Fitz," she said.

Cherubini was silent as Thompson tried to restart the engine. When she opened the driver-side door, he said: "You saw the Feds. Only so long Fitz stays free."

"I'm not interested."

"Once I'm sheriff," Cherubini said, "I'll keep you on patrol. We'll clean up this county. Police work. No more babysitting."

"Suspect in pursuit," she said. "That's all I know about police work."

"Suit yourself. *Christ*."

4

At twilight, he and Timmy hiked through the forest to the eastern wing. MacDougall knelt down on the granite floor, pressed his cheek against one of the slabs. Its coldness reminded him of the bars at Berlin Federal. *Yea, many years* since he'd been sentenced, locked up by man's law—and how long on the march?

"You know what today is?" MacDougall said.

"The last day?"

"Yes," MacDougall said. "The answer to every question since Golgotha. First let Lamp Numbers One and Two clear their accounts. When I left the Mansion, did you lead a sinful life?"

"Yes."

"Did you fall? Into the box?"

"I, uh—"

"I warned you," MacDougall said, "about the orgone accumulator. I declared it the crate of Babylon, the cage of Satan. You brought it to the Eternal Mansion. What if that box is rotting the bones of Elena Dunphy? What if she's nothing but dust?"

"Uh, I—"

"Tonight, it burns."

5

Timmy and MacDougall lifted the accumulator and laid it flat over a wheelbarrow. They rolled it to the backyard. MacDougall pried the little man's hands from his eyes and asked, "Any sign of Sarah?"

"No."

"Hammer?" MacDougall said.

"Here."

"The axe?"

"In the shed."

MacDougall squinted at Timmy. "If you can't find Jeremiah," he said, "you can at least find the axe."

In the gray evening, MacDougall examined the accumulator. A cheap thing: planks poorly cut, the hinges glued to the door. *How poorly many sold their souls.*

Timmy came out from the shed with a red hatchet.

"Blade's too small," MacDougall said.

"W-w-won't we burn it anyway?"

"Part One," MacDougall said, "is dismemberment. Swing by swing. Chop by chop. Limb by limb. Break it plank by plank. Pray until the evil leaves this once-blessed site."

MacDougall gripped the hatchet, swung, and stuck the blade in the accumulator door. He put his heel against the knob. He heaved again and strained his shoulders but could not pull it out.

"Burn it," MacDougall said. "At all times, it's eleven fifty-nine."

Timmy circled the accumulator, dousing it with gasoline. They recited the Eternal Nations creed:

We believe in

one God
the father of Abraham
Old Man on the Mountain
who brought the land
to Elena
and brought Jerusalem
to New Hampshire
We believe in
one Lord
King of Kings
our savior
until the coming of Elena
She is the Lamb of God
and lies with the Lion
she dies
and rises again
to bring the New Jerusalem
to New Hampshire
We believe
in the Holy Spirit
in the woods
of our prophet Elena
We believe
she is the Lamb
and will rise again
with the Holy Spirit
who brings Jerusalem
to New Hampshire

"Enough," MacDougall said. "Time for the exorcism."

He heard a shot fired down the ridge; a bullet hit the accumulator door.

"Get down," he told Timmy.

Timmy dropped flat on his stomach, sucked his fingers. MacDougall loaded his gun behind a line of firs.

6

A bullet snagged MacDougall's right shoulder. Clasping his elbow, he staggered back behind the trees. It had stung—*verily*—yet the projectile passed clean through his flesh.

He crawled to the summit on his belly. When he reached the top of the hill, MacDougall fired down the slope as the gunman reloaded. The third bullet hit the sniper's right leg. MacDougall marched down the ridge, his Ruger aimed at the man's groin.

"Drop the long arm," he said.

"Fuck you."

MacDougall shot his left knee.

"It could be easier," MacDougall said. "Who sent you—Fitz?"

"Yes, goddamn it," the man said.

7

"If you want to shoot me," Levesque said, "shoot me. Stop waving a gun in my face."

"I'm not going to shoot you," MacDougall said. "Timmy will shoot you."

8

A rustle of leaves came from the hill. "Might be vermin," MacDougall said.

Timmy took out his flashlight and went up the footpath. Below a large beech, one of MacDougall's traps had been sprung. He half-expected to find a squirrel or a red fox. When Timmy peered down the hollow, he saw Fitzroy.

"F-Fitz?"

"Quiet," Fitzroy whispered. He rubbed his ankle. "I'm resting."

"B-but—"

"I came to save you. I can't do it if MacDougall finds me... Understand?"

"What's going on up there?" MacDougall said.

"It's a r-r-raccoon," Timmy said.

"Leave the beast," MacDougall said. "It's eleven fifty-nine. Time for your manhood."

"Take it, son."

"You s-sure about this?" Timmy said.

MacDougall handed him the gun. *"Behold, he became as the second lamp of Revelation."*

"I c-can't kill him."

"Of course—Of course, you can kill him. This worm? Takes less than a second. What does a second matter next to eternity? It's a little leap of faith, son. Become Lamp Number Two."

"N-N-No."

"He's a worm."

Timmy stared at the ground.

"Shoot him," MacDougall said.

His fingers trembling, Timmy dropped the gun in the dirt. "W-Why does it h-h-have to be me?"

"Because it's your time," MacDougall said. "Because you're *Lamp Number Two*. Because he's a *worm*."

"I can't—"

The bounty hunter heaved forward to grab the Ruger. MacDougall knelt down, picked up the gun, and shot him twice in the forehead.

"See that?" he said.

MacDougall handed the dead man's rifle to Timmy. "Go to your room," he said. "Watch the window. See the sheriff, shoot—no excuses."

Timmy ran the dirt path to the backyard. Why, MacDougall thought, does God send the weakest men? Always traitors—Silver Pieces Man, never the Rock.

He heard Elena's voice. *Did Peter never deny the Lord?*

"Was it wrong? You're saying it was wrong to dismiss Timmy?"

The Lamb is love. Only the world is loveless, heartless. Only the world is only bowels.

"He disobeyed."

Silence.

"You're right," he said. "It doth not befit the Lamb to treateth so his little man. I submit myself to Him. As Lamp Number One, I'd have a sign."

He heard a gunshot.

10

MacDougall opened the door to the orgone accumulator. Timmy's limp body slid off the chair. He had shot himself with the rifle. All over the metal plates were pieces of brain and skull.

"Are you testing me?" he said.

Silence.

"I would have a sign."

No answer.

"A *sign*."

Nothing.

11

MacDougall sat before Timmy, clasped his hands together. He petitioned the Almighty: *The Lord is good, He hath taken me from the bottomless pit up to the light. Now He asketh me to raise the dead.*

He addressed Timmy's body. "I've given you hope, love, guidance, spirit. An earthly father. If the Lord deemeth it fit—if the Lord granteth me the power, I, Alexander MacDougall, prophet of Causeway, leader of the Eternal Nations, shall raiseth thee, Timmy Griggs, from his earthly grave."

MacDougall closed his eyes. He felt the stirring of an eternal power: an itch in the scalp, quickness of breath, tightening of loins.

From the Lord, to the hands of the prophet, to the heart and lungs of Timmy, would come the touch of life. The heart received the spirit; the spirit flowed through the veins; it flowed from his fingertips to Timmy's flesh.

MacDougall pressed his palms against Timmy's chest.

He felt the power. It warmed his legs. The warmth went up his neck and shoulders. He had never felt this force: never in Boston, never at Causeway, never at Berlin Federal. He was weightless, as though he had left his body and drifted up to the sky.

It made him laugh; he couldn't believe it. The power had arrived.

MacDougall looked down at the half-head of Timmy, who did not look any lighter, and certainly did not float.

He pumped both hands over Timmy's heart.

"Breathe," he said. "Breathe, little man."

It was no use.

Timmy was dead.

NINETEEN

1

Around the side of Causeway, the smell of gasoline wafted through the air, drifting over the yard from the orgone accumulator.

MacDougall stood on the back porch. "Want a look?"

"Where's Timmy?" Sarah said.

"The box." MacDougall nodded at the accumulator. "Open the door, greet your son."

Sarah pulled the latch. When she saw the corpse, she screamed and threw herself on Timmy's body.

"Timmy's in hell," said MacDougall.

"Monster."

"No," MacDougall said. "There's no mortal hand in this death. It's God's work... Timmy lost his nerve serving the Nations. He wept, he ran, he died. That's Timmy's story."

"Just kill me."

"Not a chance," MacDougall said. "The Lord has a plan, Sarah. This is His work. You see—this Ruger, it's not mine. I never wanted to point a gun. He put it in my hand. Did not Jesus say, 'I come with a sword'?"

He stepped down from the porch. MacDougall got close to Sarah and nudged her spine with the pistol. "Take the robe."

"I'm not—I'm not touching him."

"I tried to raise him," he said. "There are some *things* you and I have in common, which you'll learn tonight. Takest thou the robe."

MacDougall pulled the right sleeve from Timmy's arm, then the left. Bits of brain were stuck to the terry cloth.

"Now," he said, and slipped her hand into the sleeve.

"Can you feel it?" he said. "Feel the power?"

He closed the door. "See these matches," he said, "All that's left is lighting the Lord's candle."

MacDougall handcuffed her to the back rail. She sank down in the grass and turned her face away. "Who finds it painful to live with pain," he said, "can expect nothing *but* pain. If you won't burn the shed, you'll watch. Think about the seven seals. Think Wormwood."

2

The cabinet burned and he led Sarah inside the house. They walked upstairs to Pluto's Cave, where Fitzroy had once forced his truncheon on a newly-wed and nude MacDougall.

"The deaths of Brewster and Timmy," he said, "were providence. Now you're Lamp Number Two. What's more, you're my wife. Together and only together were we meant to repent."

He chanted the Prayer of Repentance:

God in heaven
I come as a
sinner
But leave as a
clean soul
Take Thy cloth
And wipe me
Drench the rag
And soak me
Scrub every place
And scour me
I am dirty
I am filthy
I need Your hands
To hold me
The Word
To console me
When it rains fire
From heaven
And all mankind
Is burned alive

You will save me
And a small group
Of people like me...

MacDougall heard the rattle of an engine on 305. It crossed over the tracks to the Eternal Mansion—where he had now restored his marriage—and the two lamps of Revelation.

TWENTY

1

On a swollen ankle, Fitzroy brushed off the leaves and dirt. He made his way to the side of the house. One of the bedroom lights turned on and he decided to wait.

He heard Harleys on the road and knew it was Spoonie and the leftovers of the Stone Men.

"Hang back," he told them.

"Sorry, Fitz," said Spoonie. "That MacWhatever killed some brothers. Tonight he gets rammed, reamed, split wide open."

"I'm the sheriff," Fitzroy said. "The one with a badge."

Fitzroy told them to leave the dooryard. Glass shattered and he turned around to see Two Stroke run up the stairs with a Ruger P90.

His pit bull followed him.

2

Fitzroy and the bikers heard a gunshot: third floor. "Oh, that's Two Stroke," Spoonie said. "That's his rugged Ruger. That MacDougall motherfucker hits the ground right—"

The body of Two Stroke crashed through the window, rolled down the eave, and landed in the garden on the chrysanthemums. A few seconds later, he was followed by his pit bull.

"Asshole," Spoonie said. "Killed the damn dog. Tonight, and all night, he gets it slow."

Four boots on the stairs, a voice in the hall: "Where's the bastard—"

"Get in the closet," MacDougall told Sarah.

"Kill me."

He dragged Sarah across the room, then picked up the gun and hid beside the door. The Ruger held five bullets: two dead cops, two dead Stone Men, one dead Fitzroy.

Two bikers rushed into Pluto's Cave. MacDougall shot them in the back and kicked their bodies to the carpet. He shut the door, threw the bolt.

A few seconds later, the door broke in half. MacDougall saw Spoonie, the bandana-wearing, bearded aviator from the clubhouse mural, standing in the hall.

Spoonie had a shotgun. MacDougall dove to the floor. The shot blasted through the mattress and the wall. MacDougall fired, hitting him in the chest. Spoonie dropped the Mossberg. He sank to his knees, foam dripping from his beard. MacDougall put the last bullet in the back of his bandana.

He tossed the Ruger out the window and retrieved the shotgun.

Fitzroy's voice from downstairs: "Spoonie?"

"Spoonie—he'll be right there."

3

MacDougall pumped the Mossberg's fore-end. He fired and buckshot tore through the framed atlas. "Come and see," he said. "Come, see, die."

He took cover behind a balustrade. The parlor was below him. MacDougall saw Fitzroy duck between a green velvet chair and the wall.

"Never took you for a killer," MacDougall said.

"I'll make an exception."

"Good. Let's see your face."

Resting his left shoulder against the wall, MacDougall shot the chair. It burst apart in a cloud of feathers.

"Come out, fat man," said MacDougall.

He fired again and blew apart one of the end tables. His right ear rang, his shoulder burned from the sniper's bullet. "Fall asleep?"

From under the couch, blood oozed across the floor. "You back there?" he yelled. "I invited you, Fitz. Come and see, come and see—unless you're a hole."

As MacDougall moved closer to the sofa, someone tackled him from behind. He tumbled down, lost the shotgun, banged his head on the landing.

He looked up and saw Sarah run to the door.

4

From the cruiser, Thompson called to Sarah. "See Fitz in there? I heard shots. Second floor."

"Mac killed him," Sarah said, and began to sob. "He's dead, or dying, I don't know. He killed Timmy."

The parlor lit up. Through the window they saw MacDougall holding a microphone; he'd set up the karaoke machine. "This is Jerusalem," he said, his voice booming through the speaker cabinets. "This is the Kingdom. Final Night. It ends, ends, ends. Forever. Tonight, Elena Dunphy rises."

Cherubini staggered out of the car. "I'm strangling him," he said.

"A nest of snakes," said MacDougall. "A generation of vipers. A colony of Sodom. Mites. Termites. *Worms.* The Lord forgive its trespasses. May He raise the prophet, Elena Dunphy."

Deputy Thompson handed Sarah the keys. "Lock the doors and roll up the windows," she said. Thompson pulled at the bulky vest beneath her uniform. "Whatever you hear, keep the doors locked."

5

Exhausted, MacDougall put down the microphone. "Elena," he cried, "where are you?"

Silence.

"Elena?"

No answer.

"What do you want?"

Nothing.

He would find Sarah, catch her straggling down the road. But when MacDougall reached for his pistol, he saw the old deputy aiming a Beretta.

"Got you now, dumb fuck."

"Ever shot a man?" MacDougall said. "All it takes is one finger."

Thompson entered the parlor. "Where's Fitz?"

"Behind the sofa," MacDougall said. "He took a nap."

Thompson walked over to the main hall. Cherubini slid a pair of handcuffs across the floor and told MacDougall to snap.

"Ever shot a man?"

Thompson called out from the hallway: "You've got to see this."

"I need you in the parlor," Cherubini said.

"The wall's all red."

"Jody—"

MacDougall grabbed his Ruger. Cherubini's bullet missed him and broke off a corner of the mantle.

Thompson ran back across the hall, drew her gun. "Holy shit," she said. "This guy killed three bikers."

"Wish I had a gun for each," MacDougall said. He looked over at Thompson. "But I only have one."

The bullet hit her stomach. She fell to the carpet, but not before Cherubini's pistol blew a hole in MacDougall's left hand.

The old deputy's gun jammed. MacDougall said, "It's over," and shot him in the skull.

6

MacDougall's hand throbbed and bled when he picked up the microphone. "Sarah, this is your prophet. Lamp Number One. God is here, the Lamp is here. Love is here."

Had she really run down the road? Maybe she'd taken refuge at Gobelin Auto. He'd find her and flush her out. "Sarah, this is Lamp Number One—"

This is Elena.

"Where's Sarah?"

Outside.

"Yes?"

Silence.

"Where is she?"

No answer.

"Elena?"

Again—no answer.

Nothing.

Sarah heard the third gunshot and popped open the cruiser door. She crept up the gravel to the backyard. Below one of the hedges, she saw something gleaming and metallic, flashing before her under the flood lights. She recognized the serrations and the gold cross on the pommel—Mac's old knife, Jeremiah. The same knife had cut up David Dunphy. A butcher's tool. The same, the same.

She heard MacDougall: "Cold out here."

He leaned against the doorway, his face, neck and hands washed in blood. "Elena waited a long time," he said, "but she left, too. We're the only ones."

"Get out of my house."

MacDougall laughed. "I just got here."

"Did you kill Fitz?" she asked.

"He's dead," MacDougall said, "like David Dunphy. Don't forget your role—you stuck shears in David's guts, Sarah. You twisted the blades, wrenched them out. And David was alive when, for all the lies he'd told, I cut out his tongue. Scraped a little from his shin. I sliced up his calf. He passed out. I should have hung him on a hook, carved him. You ever chop off a pig's head, through the neck bone? It's a jolt. Worked up a real sweat."

"You were protecting me?"

"You need it," he said. "Ever stabbed someone?"

"No."

"You going to hand over Jeremiah, or do I take him myself?"

He moved closer to her. Sarah held the knife sideways and stabbed at his chest; he grabbed her elbow, threw her against the rail. She dropped back to the deck. A column of chairs toppled and fell on the ground as the knife skittered across the table. Four wine bottles rolled off, broke on the concrete.

Ten feet of glass lay between Sarah and the knife.

She clenched her teeth, tried to stand up, but her leg was caught in one of the chairs. As she crawled over the shards, the chair scraped against the patio floor.

"Stop," he said.

Sarah kicked. MacDougall caught the chair under his boot. When she pulled out her leg, MacDougall took two steps and put his heel over Sarah's hand.

"Thou hast put all things in possession under my feet." He crouched down and picked up Jeremiah. As he kissed the pommel, Sarah grabbed the neck of a broken wine bottle and shoved it in MacDougall's face, slicing clean through his left cheek. She ran out past the yard into the woods.

"I told all of you," he yelled after her, "you don't get to kill me."

8

MacDougall stood alone in the backyard. He was nearly blind, his face flapping in the wind: the top half of his cheek wobbled, the lower half curled back down into his mouth.

O inhabitants of Bentham County, he thought, *that maketh thy nest in the birches, how gracious shalt thou be when pangs come upon thee, the pain as of a woman in birth.*

The pangs, the pain...

He was alone.

Brewster was dead. Timmy was dead. Sarah—dead to God.

And where was God? Jesus?

Elena?

Had they forsaken him?

He was alone—completely alone.

He was alone and rotting.

He didn't want to die.

"Elena!"

But maybe he—MacDougall—was the problem. He was a lamp standing alone. And if he were alone, did the Lord wish him dead by his own hand?

Did he not recall Abraham's leap of faith? The will to sacrifice Isaac, his own son, to serve the Lord. To carve up the body, render it into *spirit*. Did he not remember Jesus, who asked why He'd been forsaken? He never asked to be spared the cross. He died the death of a common thief, on the outskirts of the city. *Yea, thereafter He conquered Death.* Yea, He rose up to heaven and harrowed hell.

The Lord wanted MacDougall—Lamp Number One—to die, so he could be reborn in the Kingdom.

Next to the ashes of the accumulator, he found the gas can. He picked it up and doused himself. MacDougall retched twice, threw the empty can on the ground. His eyes burned, his mouth burned, his face and hands burned all over.

"Does this please God?" he said.

He needed a match.

TWENTY-ONE

1

Fitzroy woke at Bentham Memorial. His his arm was hooked to a drip. He looked over to his right—on the oximeter, his pulse stable around seventy-three.

At nine o'clock, Clement and Nurse Leary visited the room.

"Glad you're awake," Clement said. "I get uneasy before they wake up. Lucky Thompson wore her vest."

2

At eleven, Fitzroy expected to see Nurse Leary but it was Dumfries.

"Breathing?" Dumfries said.

"Living."

"MacDougall?"

"Took Sarah hostage at Causeway. Went to dissuade him."

"Dissuade?"

"With my Beretta."

"MacDougall burned himself alive," Dumfries said. "Bad way to go, in my opinion."

"They're all bad," said Fitzroy.

"Some good news," Dumfries told him. "Dentiste is convalescing. He might never talk again—or want to talk, given what he's seen. He did write me a note. It said the Stone Men had been surveilling their clubhouse for a month. I saw some of the footage, and let me tell you, Fitz, it doesn't flatter your department."

"My informants."

"They're all dead—Gaucho, Spoonie, Two Stroke. We're left with the evidence. Like two kilos of meth to Gaucho at seven in the morning, fifth of January."

"I'm going back to sleep," Fitzroy said.

"Sure," Dumfries said. "Don't forget to wake up."

3

Fitzroy felt nauseated as he sat up on the bed. He pulled the IV from his arm. Leaning against the metal bed frame, he steadied his legs enough to walk.

His phone rang—Dom D'Arcy's number.

"Hello?"

"Mr. Fitzroy? Gustavo. I keep your book, and Levesque's book, too. I went to see him at Bibeault's. He was not working... Tell me where to find him. Big Dom says he is slippery, like a fish."

"Nothing personal, but I'd forget about collecting."

The sheriff limped down the hall to the lobby. The waiting area was deserted except for old Godfrey, the receptionist.

"Where are my keys?" Fitzroy said.

"In your clothes," Godfrey said.

"Where are my clothes?"

Godfrey pointed back down the hall. "Autoclave."

Fitzroy retrieved his keys and his Beretta. He left Bentham Memorial in his green dressing gown.

4

Ten minutes later, he arrived home.

In the living room, Fitzroy found signs of Patrick. Tossed drawers, ashes on the carpet, a toilet lid smashed over the couch.

Blue blanket over her legs, his mother lay awake in bed. She had a bruised right eye. A line of dried blood ran down from her nose to a small pool above her collar bone.

"You came back," she said.

"Where's Patrick?"

"I told him. You locked up the pills."

"Did he find them?"

"He found me and he hit me."

Patrick tapped the muzzle of his .38 Colt against the door. "Hey, bro," he said. "Nice gown. You got fucking AIDS or something?"

"You're a disgrace."

"I need ice," Patrick said, "Bags and bags and bags. None for your little brother? That's a fucking disgrace. Gaston told me about you. All those years playing sheriff, you were dirtier than me and him and the guys on the site. No wonder your wife left. Took the kid."

Fitzroy sat next to his mother. "He's lying."

The sheriff figured he could distract Patrick before firing. He didn't care if his mother was in the room. It just had to be that way.

As he raised his leg over the blanket, two black Hondas and a van jumped the curb below the lawn. It was Dumfries and three lackeys in blue jackets.

"Time for ice," said Patrick. He raised the .38 at the door and readied himself for the battering ram. Fitzroy tapped his holster, aimed, and shot his brother twice in the back.

"W-what," his mother said.

"Business."

By the time Dumfries swept the room, Fitzroy was headed north.

5

The Caravan behind Fitzroy blew its horn—the driver, Dumfries.

His Buick hit a pothole. The car wobbled and drifted to the left, a few inches from the guardrail. As he pulled right, Fitzroy's phone rang. "Where you going, sheriff?"

"I had to see my mother."

"There's no way," Dumfries said. "I called border patrol. Turn around."

Fitzroy spat blood on the steering wheel. "Go back to Boston."

"You shoot your brother?"

"Another victim of the War on Drugs."

The Caravan blew its horn. Agent Tunnell rolled down the rear window, holding a megaphone. "We just want to talk."

Fitzroy pushed up his speed to a hundred and ten.

A few miles from Quebec, the traffic grew thicker: he passed one car, then two, then five and six. He felt lightheaded. Fitzroy turned on his siren, and his lights, too, but as he pressed the accelerator he got dizzy. His sight drained away. When his vision returned, the passenger door was skidding along the rail.

Tunnell's voice blared through the megaphone: "Think about Matty..."

To keep the Buick from rolling onto the shoulder, Fitzroy cut right. He swerved over the line and back again. To his left now lay a stretch of forest above a hillside. Fitzroy turned and ramped up.

When he reached the top, Fitzroy pulled out the brake. He left the keys in the ignition, took his gun from the glovebox, and slipped out the driver door.

"Come back, sheriff," Dumfries called to him. "We've got a blood bag."

Fitzroy ran a hundred yards through the trees. He tripped on a birch root.

He was losing blood, felt he'd already lost it all. He heard someone on the path—one person, then three, four. He heard birds, a raccoon.

"We have blood," Tunnell said.

Fitzroy wrapped his arms around the birch. The light returned to his eyes. Once more he felt his heartbeat.

He fell on his face in the mud.

TWENTY-TWO

"Ready to go home?" Thompson said.

"What was that shit?" Hank said. "Chopper—chopping..."

"A misunderstanding. Lokust and the helicopter guy took the blame. You're free to go."

"One time I saw that man," Hank said. "A skinny man. He stood on Loon Hill, a stick man stood in the wind..."

"We're all just people. I don't see the point—"

Hank rose from bench. "When I had the chance," he said, "I should have shot him. Really shot him. I could have done something with my life." He wiped his mouth, spat on the floor.

"Sarah Van Bommel moving that graveyard?"

TWENTY-THREE

1

The boat was named *L'Oiseau Bleu*. Sarah, in her green bib pants and gloves, welcomed aboard the German tourists. The day's itinerary had two hours of fishing with light casting rods, two hours of baiting and trapping lobster, and at sunset a visit to Percé Rock.

The water was rough and the Germans tangled their lines in the wind. At six, they reached the rock. "In 1607," Sarah said, "Samuel Champlain named it Percé, meaning *pierced rock*, in reference to the large holes in the limestone."

The Germans pulled down their rain-hoods. They took pictures of the enormous jutting stone, which, at a distance, looked like a ship under sail. Sarah said the villagers called it *La Génie del'isle Percé*, the phantom of the island. From its peak, northern gannets flew to the shore and to Bonaventure.

The boat returned to port. Two clouds of vapor swept over the bay. *"Kartoffeln,"* a woman said.

Suddenly Sarah felt sick. She leaned over starboard and vomited in the black water.

On the dock, Sarah got a call from Philippe.

"Papa's dead."

2

Sarah and Philippe lived in Gaspard, a village of seventy-five people above Lac Dominique. Their house was a cottage with a garret room. A wrought-iron spiral staircase joined the two floors. The downstairs was wood-paneled, and had a small bedroom, a living room, kitchen, and a bathroom with a shower.

Every day, she thought of Timmy. He'd had no funeral. Before leaving Bentham County, Sarah spread his ashes at the basin of the Sagmo.

Sarah spread the ashes alone.

On a cold October Saturday, the vigil for Luc Prévert—Philippe's father—began at ten in the morning.

The first guests were old villagers dressed in black. They shuffled inside the house and made small talk. An hour later, Laurent and Yoann arrived wearing loose serge suits. All the guests drank burgundy and so grew less somber.

At noon, the villagers of Gaspard each had a chance to speak of Luc. He was a good man, a neighbor. Someone who could fix a leaky hull or drive rats from the barn.

An old fisherman named Lefebvre said that, although Luc had never been rich, he repaid what he borrowed, and he never stole coal or eggs. Above all, he was a Christian.

Philippe brushed his teeth in their tiny bathroom and Sarah stared at him from the doorway. Over the past three years he'd gotten used to life with titanium legs; he never complained, even on drives to the Hôpital du Sacré-Coeur-de-Montréal. His doctor had given Sarah a post-op manual with illustrations of incorrect postures. The hardest part of living with Philippe was making sure he didn't lie down with his shank hanging over the bed, or sit with one leg crooked over the other. She lectured him when he sat up in the recliner.

"This the life you expected?" she said.

Philippe spat in the sink and rinsed his mouth. "Life?" he said. "You mean our life?"

"More than us. I mean, the accident—"

"No accident."

Sarah looked away from him. "Sorry," she said. "I shouldn't have brought it up."

"It's all right," he said. "It's not my legs that made me a man. If I like my life, that's enough. I don't care about the past, or old dreams. I'm a different person."

"But do you like yourself? Do you ever—"

He went to Sarah and kissed her. After taking her in his arms, he placed his hands around her stomach.

"I threw up this morning," she said. "Will it be like last time?"

"I don't know," he said. "But there is no need for fear. None, none at all."

4

Sarah looked at the field beyond the lake. Beyond it, the road stretched out to further flatness.

No mountains, no trees. Breeze over the black grass.

She'd spent her life trying to be happy. That life was over.

Her life led her to a village in the Gaspésie, rinsing out an old man's bedpan and burying him in the backyard. It had led to a new life, and to the new life inside her.

She no longer wanted to be happy.

It was a good life.

PALM SUNDAY

"Who's the exorcist for the archdiocese?"

"Silva."

"Yeah. When's he coming?"

"He can't."

"Then who'd you ask?"

"Sacred Brotherhood of Francis Borgia."

"Borgia? He'll be lucky to keep his intestines."

Maldonado stood up and went over to the table. It was spread with sweetbread, egg tarts, queijadas, and a jar of coffee milk. "I'm about to lose mine," he told Barbosa. He opened the coffee milk, sniffed it, and screwed the lid back on. "Stuff's bad. Where'd you get this?"

"Private stock," said Barbosa. "He kept it downstairs."

Maldonado picked up an egg tart and ate it. "He only stays in this house during Holy Week. That jar could be a month old."

"Figured we'd get thirsty. No use wasting good coffee milk."

"That's the whole point. It's not good."

"Want some coke?"

"The fuck does that have to do with anything?"

"I don't know. You didn't like the coffee milk—"

"So you thought I wanted coke? Jesus. How long's he been in there?"

"Ten minutes."

"Anyway—about the coffee milk. It's not that I didn't like it. It was bad. In fact, it went bad a month ago. Don't tell me I didn't like it, like it's a preference. No one could like it."

Barbosa came over and helped himself to a few of the pastries. "Should've brought some wine," he said.

Maldonado looked him in the eye. "Was Gallo really that wild?"

"Worse. Before I caught him, he burned all his clothes in the backyard. Smeared himself in shit. Said he was leaving to confess his sins."

"And you called an exorcist?"

"Why else would he say that?"

"He's dying," said Maldonado. "Few years ago he got a brain tumor. You notice he blinks a lot?"

"Get a doctor?"

"Priest. A real one, so he can read last rites."

"It's Palm Sunday. Hard enough getting an exorcist, and they do jack shit."

There was a rapping from the inside of the study door, then Father Tremblee's voice: "Could you keep it down? We're starting." The two men looked at each other, holding their paper plates. Barbosa tried not to laugh. *Vade retro satana,* Tremblee began. "For He has stripped you of your power... Cast you into outer darkness... everlasting ruin..."

"You were in the study?"

Barbosa said yes.

"You tied him down?"

"Yeah."

"Got the book?"

He frowned. "We'll get it when this is over."

"With Father Hacksaw in there? These ain't real Catholics. They amputated a guy's foot because it was speaking to them. That's why you're calling the archdiocese. I'm getting that book."

"You think Herrera wants that book?"

"Hold on. Do I think Herrera wants what?"

"The book."

"I heard you. What I can't believe is you tied him down in the fucking study and left the book. Unbelievable."

He crept to the door and found it locked. Barbosa shrugged. "I'll tell you," Maldonado said, "any man goes to Herrera with anything gets clipped."

"Clipped?"

"That's what I said. Coming back from Felt in a trash bag, with no kidneys."

"Herrera wouldn't."

"The boss turning snitch is the last straw. To be honest, Gallo's lucky he lasted. Doesn't matter if his own body kills him. When he's gone, he's gone."

"He's gone soon. And I ain't that stupid."

"Santos might be."

From the third floor, they heard murmurs on the landing. A purse dragged up the stairs. Then it began to rain.

"Did you lock the door?" said Maldonado.

It opened and the silhouette of Santos stomped in. He slammed the door shut and locked it in two places.

"Lord loves a leper," mumbled Barbosa.

"There's a crowd on the stairs," Santos told them. "All them bothered velhas."

"Think they'd bother you?" said Maldonado. "Left half your face on the pillow."

Santos took off his jacket and hung it over one of the chairs. "What do they want?"

"Who?"

"The women on the stairs."

"That's old Joao's mother, and I heard Mrs. Goncalves. They're worried if Gallo goes, so does the bagman."

"Oh."

"You got a haircut," Barbosa said.

"Yeah, job interview. Tired of the parking lot bit."

"Interview? You stripping at Cadillac's now?"

"Must be selling his dandruff." Maldonado gave him a squint: "Cops outside?"

"None that I saw."

"You looked?"

"Not really."

"Then go look. Or be condemned to watching me and Barbie eat these queijadas."

Santos inched toward the table. With quick strikes, he grabbed the coffee milk and an egg tart and retreated to the corner.

"Put that down," said Maldonado. "Trust me, you shouldn't drink it."

Santos unscrewed the lid.

"Just look at it and think about drinking it, all right? We don't have time—"

In three large gulps, Santos swallowed the coffee milk.

"You're making a mistake."

"What, this?" said Santos, and he hurled his egg tart at Maldonado. The slender man ducked and the pastry plopped against the back of Barbosa's neck.

He turned from the window: "You leper fuck."

Santos went to his right and ran past the table into the bathroom. Barbosa chased him, but he was too slow and the latch clicked before he could reach the door. He beat his fist against it. "Once the old man gets exorcised, you're next. Prick."

"Should've brought wine," said Maldonado.

The front door opened and there appeared a man wearing a cassock. In his right hand he held a black leather satchel.

Barbosa pulled his revolver. "How'd you open a locked door?"

After closing it, the priest looked squarely at him and said, "I'm Father Marques from Saint Tarcisius. The archdiocese asked me to administer last rites to Mister Gallo."

"Who called you?" Maldonado said.

"The archbishop. He regretted he could not come personally, but today's Palm Sunday."

"Never heard of Saint Tarcisius. Is that in Gottasuckit, Rhode Island?"

"I'm not used to having pistols pointed at me. If you lowered it, I would be grateful."

"Who's outside?" said Barbosa.

"People from the neighborhood. They were curious and politely agreed to leave the house."

"Put down the gun," Maldonado said. Then he addressed Marques as though he were speaking to a child: "And you, put down the case."

Barbosa frisked him, but found nothing and went back to the window.

"If I may say something," said Marques. "Every second you detain me is a second Gallo is closer to death. You want to jeopardize his soul? Leave him to the Borgias? Why was I called in the first place?"

Maldonado glanced at Barbosa, whose attention had already drifted back to the front yard. "All right," he said. "But if the study's locked, we may need to kick it open."

"You've never been to seminary. Mister—?"

"Maldonado."

"For your friend's sake, hurry."

"Show me the host."

"What?"

"If you're performing last rites, I want to see the host."

"It's in my satchel." Marques knelt down and loosened the clasps. "You know, this one isn't mine. Got it from Father Correa..."

"Who?"

"Sorry. Herrera."

The droning of Tremblee continued in the study.

Barbosa spun around from the windowsill, but it was too late.

***

Santos heard four shots and a door kicked open. He stood on the toilet seat and peered out the window. It was three floors from where he stood to the ground. The drainpipe ran on the other side of the house, far out of reach. Then came a pounding from across the hall and another gunshot. The crowd below the porch began to swell; soon the police would arrive.

The coffee milk had started to nauseate him. After placing his back to the wall, he threw the latch. One more shot, followed by the breaking of glass, and then Santos saw an enormous hulking Gallo strangling a priest. They stepped toge ther back towards the buffet table and fell over it. As he got closer, Santos saw Gallo's skin was light blue and he was foaming at the mouth. The boss gave nothing more than a few grunts while throttling the priest, who fired another shot through Gallo's stomach to seemingly no effect.

From the priest came a thin gravelly rasp, almost a hiss. Gallo moved his head to the side of his neck and bit off his ear. The priest's legs kicked out a few times before Gallo collapsed on him and they stopped moving.

He saw Barbosa and Maldonado dead on the floor; the exorcist, in his purple stole, lay with his head smashed open. From Maldonado's boot he took a knife, cut off a few of Gallo's fingers, and pocketed the rings. He slipped out the wallet and in Gallo's jacket, which he recognized as Barbosa's, found the black book.

Herrera could use it. And maybe he'd been right about Gallo slipping. There were plenty of opportunities with a new boss. Hadn't Herrera bought the Felt Club downtown? They listened to him on the Hill like they'd never listened to Gallo.

Santos fled down the stairs. The crowd was gathered by the street, so Santos went to the basement and out the bulkhead.

He'd parked the Nissan two blocks away. It was warm in the early afternoon. He watched families leaving the church down the street, the children clutching their palm leaf crosses, and he thanked God for His everlasting mercy.

MOLTING

At three in the morning, the phone beeped—my brother Darren.

"I have work tomorrow," I said.

"It's tomorrow now, little man."

He'd recently left prison and lived at a half-way house in Cambridge. It was the fifth call in four days.

"You need money?" I said.

A few seconds of wheezing. "Didn't ask for money," Darren said. "I wanted to speak to my brother. About a venture."

"Why me?"

"The other brother's dead. Asshole."

It was true. Our father had bludgeoned Frank and told the police he fell down the stairs. An accident. Darren corroborated the statements. Back then, we were six and seven—Irish twins.

Now Darren said his friend Murdo *worked at the airport...*

"Goodbye."

Right away, he rang back.

I turned off the phone.

I was a social worker, driving out to projects in Southie, Roxbury, Charlestown. At a complex like Orchard Grove, the dirtiest units had bedbugs. I kept a crowbar and protective kit in the trunk: boots, tape, wet wipes, coveralls, folding chair, latex gloves, contractor bags. Most valuable was the icing spatula, which flattened the bastards against the wall.

One morning I traveled to meet new clients—the Walshes—who had reported an infestation. In those places, the first thing you noticed was the smell: ashtrays, cat piss, and rancid butter.

"You the doctor?" Robert Walsh said.

"No," I said, holding a metal clipboard. "I'm here to take pictures and report to housing."

"About what?"

"Concerns you might have."

"Concerns," Walsh said. He sank back into the fake leather chair. "My wife's mail keeps getting stolen. And the doc's supposed to give her a new script."

"What illness?"

"Heart murmur," he said. "Replaced one of her valves. That's why she can't work no more."

"Do you work, Mister Walsh?"

"Here and there," he said. "I have friends. What you can show housing," he said, pointing to the wall, "is *that*."

Beside the door was a large spot of crushed bedbugs. A boy stood next to the wall, bitemarks on his wrists and the left side of his neck.

"How long has he stood there?" I said.

"All morning," Walsh said. "Brian, show the man."

Brian slapped his palm against the dried blood and made circles, as though he were buffing cars.

"Is he your son?"

"My wife's," Walsh said. "All I can do is feed him."

I asked where he'd seen insects.

"Front room, halls, bedrooms…"

"More than one?" I said. "The apartment's listed as a single."

He shrugged. "We sort of improvised."

"Where does the boy sleep?"

"In my room." The voice belonged to a young woman, who looked more like a college student than she did an Orchard tenant. Below her long brown hair, she wore jeans and a cream cardigan.

"What's your name?" I said.

"Rose."

"My stepdaughter," Walsh said. "Moved back when her ma got sick."

"Where'd you live?"

"Springfield," she said.

Rose brought me to the bedroom. I noticed scuff marks on the floor, an arc from doorway to dresser.

"What were you doing in Springfield?" I said.

"Living with a guy."

"Do you feel safe here?"

"My mom needs me."

"You need that dresser," I said. "Why was it pressed against the door?"

Rose lounged on the comforter. I squatted in front of her, clipboard across my lap. "Does your stepfather drink?"

"Every night."

"How much?"

"Robert's always been this way," she said. "It's his smack my mother bought. Blew out her heart."

"What about your brother?"

Outside her mother coughed and coughed. Brian squealed.

Walsh pounded on the door.

"My card," I told Rose. "Call if it gets worse."

3

Darren sounded like he'd been awake all week.

"Brother..."

"What is it?" I said.

"They're letting the men inside," he said. "At night."

"Men?"

"Little men with red hair. Red faces. When they get angry, they shed their skins. I threw one out the window."

I yawned. "But why'd you call?"

"Listen, you prick—I got something to say."

"Like what?"

"I'm out."

I got up and went to the window. "Where are you?"

"Here, there," he said. "I'm on a venture."

From the alley, I heard barks and a chain rattle against the fence. Then it sounded over the line.

"Don't be stupid," I said. "Go back to the house."

"Burned it down."

"Bullshit."

Another bark.

"Those aren't *your* dogs," I said.

"It's my goddamn money," Darren said, "when I sell them. Know what real breeders charge?"

Keep watching from the window.

I wasn't sure if I'd said it, or Darren.

4

Something smelled rotten above the office at Orchard Grove. When the manager opened the apartment door, I covered my nose and hustled downstairs to the street.

The body was a retired nurse's—a hoarder who died under a pile of phonebooks. The medics said her face melted in the heat. At first, it had been impossible to tell if the corpse was male or female.

That night I drank two bottles of wine: one for the nurse, one for her face.

At midnight, I received a call.

"Mister McCarthy?" Rose said. "I was hoping you could help me."

Once she stopped crying, I said I'd visit the building with a police officer.

"No," she said. "They'll stick Brian in foster care. I know what it's like."

In the morning, we met at a café downtown. Rose arrived late, dragging a tattered umbrella. Her hair and cardigan were wet.

"I never leave Orchard Grove," she said.

"Less than you should."

I ordered coffee; Rose, nothing. When she wept, I offered a napkin. Rose reached over the table and grasped my sleeve.

"It's not company rules," I said, "but if you need a place to stay..."

"You mean it?"

I placed my other hand on hers.

We spent the day around the city. I looked like a Tremont Street john as we strolled by the Common. "Does your stepdad get out?"

"Beer and scratch tickets," Rose said. "Robert can't drive. He'd never walk this far from the courtyard."

We went to my place, where I gave her an oversized black t-shirt and a pair of sweatpants. She rolled them above her knees.

"You don't do drugs," she said. "Do you?"

I shook my head.

"Drink?"

"Sometimes," I said.

"Anything here?"

In the cabinet was a bottle of Gran Marnier, unopened and coated in a film of dust. We sat on the couch sipping it at room temperature.

"Can I smoke?"

"It isn't allowed," I said. "The clerk is nosy. He gawked at you downstairs."

"Reminds me of Robert," she said. "Loaded every night. He watches porn loud enough for the neighbors."

"Then he creeps to your room?"

"He used to stand outside and sing. Disgusting songs... When mom got sick, he said I was the woman of the house. I had responsibilities."

I asked if he'd hurt her.

"Springfield was worse," she said. "I can't remember the last time someone was nice to me."

"I'm different."

"You must see horrible things."

"Most of the time," I said, "it doesn't feel like I help anyone. Like making an endless snuff film."

"I'm not dying," Rose said. She downed her glass. "Neither are you."

5

The bedbugs multiplied at Orchard Grove.

"Goddamn trash piles," the manager said, waving at the mounds of garbage around the dumpster. "Some are from the residents. Some are from guys in shades and thousand-dollar jackets."

After lunch, I discovered a client's laundry bag under my backseat. I snapped on latex gloves and cut it open. Among the hair-covered blouses and soiled underwear were three small dots. I crushed the bugs with a wet wipe. Afterwards, I collected feces and molted nymph skins. Any relief I felt left during self-inspection: below my ear were another two.

6

There was a guest at my place. He shook hands with a pubic hair in his hangnail.

Rose said, "This is Gavin."

"From Springfield?" I asked.

They were high school friends, hadn't seen each other in years.

I made an excuse and went to the bathtub, where I scoured my neck and legs with steel wool. Over the running water, Rose giggled. The front door slammed.

"Let me know," I told her, "if you plan on having people over. This apartment—"

"Might be infested," she said. "Did you think about me? About bringing *me* here?"

"You're clean."

"How would you know?"

I'd meant to buy wine. The bottle of Gran Marnier was half-full.

"Let me look," she said, turning down my shirt collar. "Nothing here."

Rose kissed me and placed my hand on her breast.

7

I picked up the phone at quarter to three—low moans.

"I know it's you," I told Darren. "Speak."

My calves and armpits itched. I flung the blanket across Rose's hip. "Don't you know what to do?" I whispered. "One thing left."

The moaning stopped.

"Kill yourself," I said. "What's keeping you?"

"You."

"Not anymore. Since when did we care about each other?"

Darren said, "I didn't kill Frank."

"How old was he?"

"Five."

"And what happened?"

"He fell down a flight of stairs," Darren said.

"You were always a bastard," I said. "You've gotten worse."

That afternoon I bought a bottle of merlot, only to find Rose had been drinking for hours. On the table was a pint of vodka and several half-smoked joints. I wrapped them in a paper towel. "These from Gavin?"

"Thought you wanted to help."

While I poured vodka in a coffee mug, she grabbed the wine: "We'll need it."

I settled down at the table—chipped IKEA. If Rose was going to stay, we'd need a nicer set.

"You're good to me," she said. "Why?"

"Well—"

"Because of Frank?"

"You heard all that?"

"Some," she said.

The merlot put me to sleep. Sometime around three, a light beamed in from the hall. There were two voices: one was Rose's.

I got up. From behind the doorway, someone hit my head with a claw hammer. I dropped down as blood poured between my fingers.

What seemed like hours later, the clerk poked my ribs.

"All right?" Selinger said.

I groaned and tapped the floor.

"Should I call an ambulance?"

"No."

"Would you mind going inside?"

Selinger pulled me into the living room, where I was dropped on the sofa. I heard him scrubbing up the blood. At one point, he kicked over the bucket and cursed. Soapy water ran under the door as I drifted off.

8

I taped my forehead with gauze and scanned the apartment for bedbugs. Below the window were several—I crushed them with the spatula. When I returned to wipe up the shit and molted skins, they had jumped to the wall. I scraped them off with my bare hands and ate them.

The next few days were spent in bed. Then came a knock.

"Police."

"It's open," I croaked.

Footsteps of three men swept over the entrance—one of them, judging by the cobbled wingtips, was Selinger.

"That's him," he said. "In and out, he brings women. Some kind of pimp."

The inspector dragged a chair. "Spoke to your brother recently?"

"Why?"

"You were named," he said, "in Darren's suicide note. Did he mention harming himself?"

"No."

"Nothing at all?"

"I mentioned it," I said. "I told Darren to blow his brains out."

This startled the inspector. For some reason, I laughed.

"That's a serious admission," he said.

"Don't believe this pimp," said Selinger. "His women bring strange men. I refuse to work a desk in Gomorrah."

I laughed even louder as they left.

Now bugs were everywhere: floor, ceiling, carpet, cushions. When I brandished the spatula, they scattered. What could I do but toss my belongings? Blankets and cushions were sealed in bin liners and launched from the window. Chairs went, as well as bookshelves and the chipped IKEA. The sofa was too big. I gave up and visited the Walshes.

9

Robert Walsh, sitting with a Coors, watched his horse race.

I hoisted the crowbar. "Where's Rose?"

With his white tongue, Walsh said, "She's not here. If she walked through that door, I'd give it to her."

"That's why she came to me."

"To—you?"

I had a three-foot reach advantage and used it on Walsh's shoulders, knees, skull. Blood bubbled and dribbled from his nostrils as he tried to crawl away.

In the silverware drawer, I found a .38. "You were going to shoot me?" I said. "For killing your fucking pests?"

The moronic titter was Brian's. He opened his hand, caked with bug guts. "Want some?" he said. "They're free."

My stomach was sick; I turned to the sink.

Brian said, "She's hiding."

"In her room?"

He rubbed his hand against his shorts as I entered the hall. Beyond Rose's door, bedsprings creaked. "Your stepdad," I said, "is flesh and blood. Not all of him's left."

On my third attempt, the dresser crashed to the floor.

Rose said, "You weren't invited."

I dropped the crowbar. "That was the point," I said. "He's dead. He can't hurt you anymore."

"Is that what you thought?"

She knocked away my hand.

"Don't," she said. "I can't stand when you touch me."

I went back to the living room. Brian stared at Walsh's battered face.

"Is he hungry?" the boy asked.

I held the revolver and looked at my left hand. Eight shots in the cylinder: I could even miss.

My thumb went easy.

10

After a month at Lemuel Shattuck, I was arraigned and jailed at South Bay.

One day—Rose.

We met behind glass in the visitation room. She wore knee boots and a green jacket with plaid lining. Next to her stood Brian, so clean as to be unrecognizable.

"Get me out of here," I said. "Tell them what happened."

"My mother died."

I restrained myself. "Sorry for your loss."

"Are you?" Rose said. "She died in pain. More than you'll ever know."

I raised my stump of a hand. "The police said you contradicted me."

"With the truth."

Like a child, I broke down. The first time I'd cried in front of Rose.

"I came to say thanks," she continued. "Because of you, we're free."

Gavin entered the room. Brian sprinted over and hugged him.

"I have to go," Rose said.

Spots formed on the glass. She kissed Gavin on the cheek. I tried gripping the receiver with my withered lump.

My time was up.

I didn't kill Frank, I heard.

I wasn't sure if it was me or Darren.

BLAST AND CRUISE

Mikey Conlan pounded the bottom of his fist against the wall. Someone next door at the Granada was throwing a party, laughing and opening bottles and playing house music all morning.

"Some of us," he yelled, "are here doing business. I'm doing business, for God's sake."

Shayla put down her beer in the sink. "They're not listening."

Mikey took a step back from the radiator, turned on the ball of his right foot, and drove his knuckles through the drywall. He wrenched out his dust-covered arm, inched closer to the window, and punched another hole. After the third, the music stopped and the room fell silent.

Mikey slumped down on the edge of the bed. "Give me a drink, I need to call my son."

"For what?" Shayla said.

"Why you asking what? It's his birthday."

Mikey reached his ex-wife's voicemail: "Hi Krissy . . . This message is for Jake . . . Put his ear to the phone . . . Hey Jake, it's Mikey . . . I mean, uh, your *dad* . . . Calling to wish you a happy birthday, guy. Your mom said you're having friends over at McDonalds. Your dad wants to be at McDonalds, but he has this business thing. You see, your mother asks for a *fucking lot of money* every month . . . Excuse me, it's your birthday. You shouldn't hear nothing like that . . . Catch you later, guy."

Shayla tapped her nostril and sat cross-legged on the carpet. "You tell me things," she said, "You told me it would be just us."

Mikey's skin was dry and tight, and he wished Shayla would leave the room. After the injection, he didn't want her to see him coughing on the floor for three minutes.

Mikey heard a knock on the door: "Mister Conlan?"

***

Mikey "Crusher" Conlan had been a middleweight contender for nine months. As contender he fought twice, and in the second fight, in front of his home crowd, he lost the match and most of the vision in his left eye.

A detached retina kept him from renewing his license in the United States. Mikey fought his last bout in a high school gym in Barbados, where he was knocked out in the third round.

Now none of it mattered. "Look in that bag," he told Shayla after paying off the concierge. "There's more in that duffel than I earned my whole career. Take ten twenties and go to the liquor store. Get a pack of Winstons, too."

"You let Dermot borrow the car."

"Then walk," Mikey said. "Steal a shopping cart, I don't give a fuck."

Shayla left the motel and he called Dermot: "Said you'd be back by eleven."

"On my way, champ," Dermot said. "Trouble with the cops—they want double for selling downtown."

"They shell up, I'll pick them apart."

"Remember that fight against Consuelo? High guard for nine rounds and you nailed his chin with an uppercut . . ."

"Consuelo dropped *me*," Mikey said.

He felt an itch below his nipple and stripped off his undershirt. He no longer had a boxer's body: his arms were swollen, his belly a fishbowl. After his last cycle of steroids, Mikey got depressed and almost threw himself from the roof of the Granada. This one would be different: a blast of Dianabol, Masteron, and Trenbolone, followed by a cruise with weekly testosterone to keep him calm and focused.

He decided to stretch first.

When he finished his knuckle push-ups, the door slammed open and six uniformed policemen charged into the room. Before he could reach under the pillow for his .38, Mikey felt a truncheon over his throat and then a fist to the solar plexus that dropped him to his knees.

By the time he could breathe again, the handcuffs cut into his wrists and the cops were prodding his lower back with the truncheon. He looked up and saw Dermot, hands in his pockets, talking to one of them.

"You fuck," Mikey said.

"Hey, champ, I got a kid."

"So do I."

Sergeant Regan wore a black jacket with his badge around his neck. He took out a roll of twenties from the duffel and counted them. "Hey Dermot," he said, snapping off his latex gloves, "maybe an extra two for your trouble."

"You mean it?"

"No."

The men around him laughed. One said, "Hey, what about me? I lost a grand on the Consuelo fight."

"We'd be paying off every cop in the state . . ."

***

"Can I blast?"

"No."

"I need a blast," he told Regan. "Goddamn it, I missed my shot."

"Gear's in evidence. Money, too. Most of it."

"Please."

"You know what," Regan said to the driver, "let's give Crusher a dose."

The car headed west, driving through quiet neighborhoods of triple-deckers. They went past Mikey's old gym and down a tree-lined access road to a garage.

"No blood on my bike," the driver said. He was a foot taller than Mikey and twice as big. "I just paid it off."

"Put a tarp on it."

"No tarp."

"Take him to the river."

The river was a thirty-foot drainage ditch. When they finished, they rinsed Mikey's hair in the brown water and dragged him back to the car.

"Now he'll be quiet," said the driver.

His good eye was blind and he sat with his split nose pressed against the window. The old Taurus swung left, left, and again left. Regan said, "Hey, is that Shayla with the shopping cart?"

Mikey pounded his head against the glass until he passed out.

APOCALYPSE CONFIDENTIAL IS

Jacob Everett..*Publisher & Editor-in-Chief*

Brendan McCauley...*Visual Arts Editor*

Max Thrax...*Managing Editor*

Tom Will..*Poetry Editor*

D.A. Wohler...*Fiction Editor*

Eitan Zion..*Essays Editor*

Tully K..*Editor-at-Large*

Rachael Haigh..*Director of Operations*

Will Waltz..*Books Editor*